PSYCH PROBE

The last unit to enter the crime scene was the psych probe. They would construct the holographic crime scene that the investigators could walk into and look around in, a scene based on a detailed workup of a victim. Brackett and Daily stood watching them work, amazed and humbled as always. The psych probe team were the true unsung heroes of Star Precinct 107.

Morgan, the chief of the psych probe unit, came out to talk to Brackett and Daily. "That's sure as hell a mess in there," Morgan said.

"I just wonder what the killer plans to do with the ears and eyes and hands," said Daily.

"We've run into an awful lot of cannibalism lately," Morgan said . . .

STAR PRECINCT
The electrifying new series by
KEVIN RANDLE
author of the _Jefferson's War_ series
and RICHARD DRISCOLL

STAR PRECINCT
MIND SLAYER

KEVIN RANDLE
AND
RICHARD DRISCOLL

ACE BOOKS, NEW YORK

I would like to thank our editor, Peter Heck, who made writing this novel not only pleasant but instructive as well.

—RD

Chapter One

The gunfighters moved slowly toward each other up the hushed, dusty street. Scruffy men and fallen women stood under the overhangs of the saloon and the hotel to watch the fatal shoot-out, which was about to take place. There hadn't been a quick-draw contest like this since the days of Dodge City and the Ringo Kid.

Now, each gunfighter dropped his hand closer to the butt of his .44. The shooting would start any time now in the curious silence of this sun-scorched old town.

There was nothing special about the villain. He wore the standard black costume—hat, shirt, pants, boots, all a dusty ebony—as well as the standard mustache and snarl.

It was the hero who looked somewhat peculiar, standing just over seven feet tall, his entire body covered with a peach fuzz, which appeared green in the harsh sunlight. In his white hat, shirt, pants, and boots the mighty Obo, a humanoid from Tau Ceti, was in no danger of being mistaken for either Roy Rogers or Hopalong Cassidy.

The men stopped suddenly, the pointed toes of their boots finding the X marks that had been drawn in the dirt. They were to fire from here.

"You ready, you low-down owlhoot?" Obo said, straining to remember the three lines the shoot-out guide had given him.

"Ready any time you are, you varmint," the villain

said. He didn't have any trouble remembering his lines. He was an android. He'd been programmed for all this.

"Then draw, you egg-suckin' tinhorn!" Obo said. So far, this had been his favorite part of the whole experience—even more than the fancy costume— saying the words "egg-suckin'."

Bart, the villain, went for his gun.

Obo, the Tau Ceti, went for *his* gun.

Gunfire roared and smoked on the morning air. Most of the onlookers headed for cover.

Amid all the noise, a human cry was heard. Bart had been shot. Fatally. He fell over backward with greased precision, the back of his skull hitting the skull-mark X in the dust exactly.

Obo, spurs jangling, .44 smoking, went up to the body and looked down, pushing back the wide brim of his ten-gallon white hat with the barrel of his weapon.

"This town is safe again for the good folks," Obo said.

And then he turned and looked back at the school-marm and the minister and the sweet plump little woman who ran the orphanage.

They were cheering him.

Obo, and this wasn't in the script at all, got a lump the size of a baseball in his furry throat.

It felt good to be a hero, even if you were seven feet tall and the color of a slightly spoiled lime.

It felt darned good.

Brackett was in the casino coffee shop, trying to negate the effects of a hangover with a good break-fast. The breakfast was losing the contest. Badly. Over the years he'd tried the most popular brands of hangover pills but while they cured the hangover they produced the undesirable side effect of turning his bladder into a sieve. No, he just had to suffer.

Lieutenant Richard Brackett was a star cop, a detective inspector, to be exact. Until his late thirties, he'd been a criminal and a bad one. But then one of the Bracketts' sleazy friends killed Brackett's wife, and Brackett, after beating the man to death with his fists, decided to work for the other side. Without revealing his background, he offered himself to the star force. Despite his occasional belligerence, and despite his lack of impressive formal education, Brackett had achieved the rank of full detective inspector within five years—a notable task by any standard. And, as he sometimes told himself in his mirror, he looked damned good in the handsome gray uniform that went with the job.

He sipped more coffee and looked around.

Tumbleweed was a vacation planet in the Artnian sector. The motif was that of a dude ranch. In other words, it was a place where people got to imagine they were cowpokes and cowpokettes in the Old West. Also, it was a great way to meet members of the opposite sex—or sexes, depending on your species.

Now, checking out the coffee shop, Brackett saw what a hub-of-the-worlds Tumbleweed really was. Creatures of every description were crowded in here. Some were purple, some had a whole row of eyes, some had wiggly stalks sticking out of their ears, some had big froglike wind sacs growing from their backs. Some were gorgeous, such as the elfin ladies of the planet Remar, with their golden eyes and breathtaking humanoid bodies, and others were repulsive. He'd never get used to the Krogans and their cannibalistic habit of chomping on their own flesh as a meal. The sight (and sounds) of this process was nauseating in an otherwise civilized coffee shop.

Hearing a voice from behind that reminded him of a bassoon, he knew that Obo and Sergeant Jennifer Daily had returned from Obo's early-morning gunfight.

The duo slid into the other side of the booth and said good morning, both taking note of Brackett's eyes.

"Stayed pretty late at the casino, huh?" Daily said, trying hard to keep any hint of amusement from her voice. Sure she'd graduated third in her class at the academy and sure she was a young, gorgeous red-head and sure she was a very decent and very chari-table person—but given even this kind of edge, she was no match for her superior officer when he had a hangover.

"Later than I should have," Brackett said, picking up his coffee cup.

"Well, I killed Bart," Obo said, smiling, "and the schoolmarm gave me a kiss." He glanced at Daily. She was smiling too.

Brackett liked the big humanoid. There was a male sweetness about him you didn't expect to find in somebody who could destroy most people with a single punch. "I'm glad you had a good time, Obo. Sorry I let you down. But when I got up . . ." Brackett shrugged.

Obo laughed, really sounding like a bassoon now. "I remember. Remember on Deneb IV?" Obo had re-cently started taking deep-hypno implants to help perfect his pronunciation of English. The implants were working. He spoke virtually without accent.

"I remember," Brackett said, smiling. The specta-cle of the big green giant walking around with an ice pack tied to his head was pretty comic.

Daily didn't have a lot of tolerance for small talk, and she'd plainly had enough. "Do we search his cabin this morning?" she said.

"Daily is tired of our palaver," Obo said.

"So I gather," Brackett replied, wishing Daily could be a little better with her segues. Brackett wasn't particularly sensitive, but Daily's way of changing the subject always vaguely hurt his feelings and made him feel foolish.

"So, do we try his cabin this morning, Lieutenant?"

Brackett sighed, knowing the time for business had arrived whether his head and stomach were ready or not. "Yes," he said, "as a matter of fact we do."

"Did we get an inspection warrant?" Daily said.

"Not as far as I know."

"Then you realize, sir, that we'll be breaking the law when we enter his cabin."

"Yes, Daily, I realize that."

"You know what Captain Carnes would say about that."

"Oh, yes," Brackett said, "yes, I'm well aware of what Captain Carnes would say about that."

Captain Jason Carnes was Brackett's immediate superior. He came from five generations of star cops and was well connected politically. He looked on the rough-hewn Brackett as something of an embarrassment to the corps.

"But you're going to do it anyway?" Daily said.

Brackett nodded. "With or without you, Daily."

Obo said, "Technically, Jennifer, what Brackett has in mind isn't strictly against the law."

Daily frowned. "This should be good."

Obo spread his massive hands. "Very simple. Motif worlds such as this one aren't full members of the Federation, even though we do acknowledge them as having full constitutional guarantees. But occasionally we bend the laws a little bit, when we really feel it's necessary."

Daily was a strict believer in law and order. She was not about to be mollified. "So we break into someone's cabin, steal the book he's writing, and then arrest him with evidence gathered illegally.

That sure isn't the way the academy said it would be."

Brackett laughed. "God, Daily, we're trying to help somebody, not hurt somebody."

"What's going to get hurt here is the letter of the law."

Brackett and Obo looked at each other and shook their heads. Daily could be stubborn as hell. Why did she have to go and be so high principled, anyway? Couldn't she be a little sleazy, like Brackett?

Or like Wade Foster, the "Saddle Pard" whose hour-long TV show was the most popular in the Federated worlds. Sure, it was an old-fashioned Western, with shoot-outs every ten minutes, but with oddball creatures from the outreach worlds playing the villains, it was the state of the art in old-fashioned Westerns.

But TV star Wade Foster was having problems. For the past two years, Foster had been a recruiting spokesman for the police corps. Now an exposé scribe named Dirk St. Romaine was going to publish a book accusing Wade Foster not only of being addicted to stardust (an outreach drug in vogue with vid stars) but a sexual pervert as well. St. Romaine planned to accuse Foster of sleeping with an outreach creature called the Dazzler, a sea being that could wrap itself about you like an octopus. While nearly killing them—its partners had to learn how to escape its clutches or perish—the creature gave Terrans the biggest sexual thrills of their lives. It was said that once you had carnal knowledge of the Dazzler— which was, by the way, a highly illegal being in the Federated worlds—you'd never again want anything to do with Terran sex, straight, gay, whatever.

This was the sort of charge that could end a career, not to mention bring shame to the corps. After all, Wade Foster was their spokesman. Still, Brackett supposed, even though he'd been charged with finding out exactly what St. Romaine had on Foster, the corps wouldn't want him to break any laws getting it. Which was why Tumbleweed was working out so nicely. As Obo said, Federation law didn't strictly apply here.

"Anyway," Daily said, "how do we even know he brought his material here?"

"St. Romaine has a reputation as a blackmailer and an extortionist," Obo said. "He knew that Foster was coming to Tumbleweed for a vacation. St. Romaine will probably offer to sell the material to Foster for a considerable amount of money."

"So we grab the material before he can offer it for sale," Daily said.

"Exactly," Brackett said.

She was softening, but just to show that she hadn't lost all her ethics, she said, "This still isn't the way the academy would prefer to see it done."

"No, but then the academy probably wouldn't prefer to see somebody like St. Romaine prey on innocent victims."

"Who said Foster was innocent?" Daily said.

"Well, relatively speaking," Brackett said, laughing.

"God," she said, shuddering. "Do you really think he let a Dazzler . . . ?"

"Apparently so," Brackett said.

"All those poor little kids," Obo said.

"What poor little kids?" Brackett said.

"The ones who watch his show. The ones who look up to him. The ones who idolize him."

"Oh, yeah, right."

"Stardust and a Dazzler," Daily said. "The man is a pervert for sure."

"Well," Brackett said, standing and getting his credit coin ready to feed into the meter on the far end of the table. The meter calculated not only the bill but the tip, too. "Let's go bail our favorite pervert out of trouble."

"He isn't *my* favorite pervert," Daily said.

"Oh, no? Then just who *is* your favorite pervert?" Obo said.

"Very funny, Obo."

"Lighten up, Daily," Brackett said.

"Yes, I guess I should be happy, shouldn't I? We're going to trample on some poor man's inalienable constitutional rights, and I guess I should be downright overjoyed, shouldn't I?"

The same look as before passed between Brackett and Obo.

No doubt about it; bright, nice, and beautiful as she was, Daily could definitely be a pain in the old backside.

They left the coffee shop and went out into the warm, bright world of Tumbleweed.

Chapter Two

Tumbleweed City was, in effect, a vast metroplex divided into two parts—the inner city, which was essentially a huge gambling town, with more than forty casinos and half as many high-rise hotels, and then the magnificent resort of Tumbleweed itself, a perfect copy of an old-fashioned Western state, complete with mountain range, desert, and three or four authentically reproduced Western towns, which sat adjacent to an impressive resort of four hundred cabins, eight swimming pools, six nightclubs, and numerous tourist shops. 'Copters worked the skies night and day, delivering tourists, removing tourists, and taking tourists on tours of the land.

Brackett, Daily, and Obo were presently 'coptering over desert. The pilot was laughing at a chase in progress below. A gambler was running from a local lawman's motorcycle. The pilot had earlier told the cops that the gambler had lost a great deal of money and had then grabbed a blaster and killed three casino guards and four vacationers. Pleasant as motif worlds were, most of them had a dark side. This was Tumbleweed's dark side—people made psychotic by gambling.

The lawman pursuing the gambler was merely playing with his prey, just waiting until he could think of something to make this death interesting. Might as well save the state an execution and get it over with out here in the desert. The lawman kept running the motorcycle up very close to the gambler;

even from up here you could hear the man's tiny cries. And then the lawman just flattened him, knocked the man down and rode right over him. "Wow," the pilot said, "somebody should have vidded that one for the news."

But the lawman wasn't done. He turned the big Harley around and came roaring back to the corpse, positioning himself for a very special run. The lawman, all got up in white hat, shirt, jeans, and boots, revved up the Harley, did a spectacular wheelie, and then bore down on the dead man.

Seeing what was about to happen, Daily turned away. Brackett watched, but without pleasure.

The lawman rode right over the man's neck, cleaving the head from the shoulders. The head shot nearly ten feet up in the air, hovered there momentarily, and then plunged back to the ground, where the lawman gave it a swift kick, as if he were playing soccer.

Obo said, "Cruelty is never pleasurable."

"Hell," the pilot said, "the poor bastard was dead anyway."

"His body was dead but not his soul." Unlike most species in the Federation, the people of Tau Ceti believed passionately in an afterlife.

The 'copter veered abruptly to the right, angling toward the desert and the mountains, which shone postcard perfect in the brassy sunlight.

Brackett reached over to Daily and tenderly patted her hand. He said nothing. There was nothing to say. Such is the way of the worlds.

Daily looked back to where the headless corpse lay but it was only a black dot on the land now, receding, receding.

Half an hour later, the three star cops were walking along a tiled veranda. To the left of them, a huge swimming pool resounded with laughter, squeals,

and shouts as a gill man from the water world of
Arnat III shot water from his elephantlike trunk
straight into the air. Terran children loved freaks,
and the gill men were among the freakiest of aliens
from the outreach planets.

The trio recognized many famous people as they
moved toward St. Romaine's cabin. Politicians and
vid stars alike came to Tumbleweed to relax, usually
with bodyguards determined to keep the press away.
A white-haired gentleman, turned pink by the sun,
lounged on a towel by the splashing blue waters of
the pool; a senator infamous for his junkets at tax-
payers' expense. No doubt his presence on Tumbleweed would be written off as "research." Not far
away, a starlet waggled her lovely behind at a group
of amateur photographers, none over eighteen, all of
whom seemed to have been rendered downright
goofy by the starlet's sumptuous body. Finally, they
saw, sitting at a patio table, the umbrella casting a
deep, cool shadow across his cowboy costume, Wade
Foster himself. He had an old-fashioned acoustic
guitar slung across his lap, and looked as if he were
posing for a still photograph. The Western hat, the
pearl-buttoned shirt with white piping, and the carefully arranged kerchief all contrived to say "hero."
Except for his expression. Even from a distance, his
face looked jowly and piqued, with narrow, forlorn
eyes. This was one cowpoke who wasn't happy. Because the three star cops were here undercover—
wearing Western clothes that marked them as
tourists—Foster didn't even glance at the trio.

Beyond the pool, the cabins started stretching up
into the foothills. To Brackett, the cabins looked like
one giant housing development, despite all their fake
"bunkhouse" accoutrements, such as a hitching post
out front. But then, Brackett was a dour man, not
known for getting into the spirit of fun activities.

Dozens of people passed them, all got up as cow-

boys, all giggling, all happy. From somewhere, a
speaker played Roy Rogers and Gene Autry songs
(Roy and Gene were on the vid Saturday mornings,
though updated with holo-depth and shimmering
color) and the odor of genuine horse shit wafted over
from the corral. What more could a guy ask for?

"How do we get in his cabin?" Daily said.

Brackett pulled out his identi-patch. This particular model, which could be obtained only by star cops
from the rank of captain or above, was given out
sparingly. "I don't think we'll have any trouble."

"What if he's at home and working?"

"Then we go back to the pool and order lemonades
and wait him out," Brackett said.

Brackett laughed. "You're bound and determined
to mess this up for me, aren't you?"

They walked on to the cabin: number 63, row B.

Fortunately, St. Romaine's place was set off from
the others in a small grove of hardwood trees, which
gave them a little bit of cover.

Brackett went right up the ten-foot walk that led
to the front door of the cabin. In the yard was a small
grill that at night vaguely resembled a campfire.
People liked to sit around and sing campfire songs.
Some people, that is. Not Brackett.

Daily said, "Wait for me, Brackett," and came running up the walk.

He was glad to have her along. He liked Daily. She
was good, and sometimes very good. Indeed, he
sometimes felt she was the best cop on the entire precinct ship.

He knocked once, twice—firm but not thunder-
ous—and then waited.

No response.

He knocked again.

Still no response.

Obo said, "Not home."

"One more time to be safe," Brackett said, and knocked once more.

"And then we just go in?"

"Then we just go in, Daily."

There was no response this time, either.

Brackett tried the doorknob. Locked. He tried the computer-controlled identi-patch. All that was necessary was a quick wave of the card, and the computer would scan it and let you in.

Brackett held up his identi-patch.

The door slid open.

Obo stepped aside, bowed, and offered them a courtly gesture meant to usher them inside. Taus delighted in parodying Terran manners.

The place was showy enough but pretty standard, featuring a completely automated kitchen, game room, and living room, which was filled with everything from a couch that rocked you like a baby to the latest in discreet and tasteful sexual appliances.

There was no sign of the writer St. Romaine.

They spent five minutes looking around, instinctively dividing the place into thirds.

And then Daily, the first to drift toward the bedroom, said, "Oh, God, Brackett. I think I found him."

For Daily to sound upset was unusual. She'd seen a lot of violence in her relatively short career.

"St. Romaine?" Brackett said.

"Yes. It's pretty bad." She shook her head. "Somebody ripped out his eyes and cut off his ears and hands. My God."

Brackett gulped. Even he was not sure he wanted to look at something like this.

But good cop that he was, he brushed past Daily and went into the bedroom.

Chapter Three

The ears had been the tough part. You'd think ears would cleave off pretty quickly. But the killer had had to use a lot of power, and saw through the bone and flesh as if sawing through the world's gristliest dinner roast.

Not that this slowed the killer down.

If there was anybody who deserved to die, it was St. Romaine. And so the killer kept up the good work. After the ears—get the tough part done first—came the eyes, which were no problem at all, and then the hands, which were a problem soon solved by use of a hand ax the killer had brought along. Thwoomp, thwoomp, and St. Romaine's hands had been reduced to two bloody stumps.

After finishing up with the actual murder, the killer started backtracking. Most killers were caught because in a moment of panic, they left something behind. Something that led the cops straight to the culprit.

No such problem here. The killer was methodical . . . going room to room, checking everything, and then checking everything again.

Then the killer left, carrying a trendy little shopping bag holding St. Romaine's ears, hands, and blue, blue eyes.

The killer spent the next two hours drinking in one of the casino bars.

This was a momentous day.

Bigger even than the day you first have sex with someone or something else; bigger even than the day you discover you're not like everybody else and must hide your secret from suspicious minds.

So the killer listened to music and drank the drinks and tried to be just like everybody else in the cool shadows of the bar.

Just like everybody else here.

But the killer couldn't be. Not quite.

After all, murderers, even in this day and age, were a pretty elite group.

Chapter Four

Brackett was talking to a dead guy. Or trying to, anyway.

The so-called Steelman Probe allows the interrogation of the victim if (a) he or she hasn't been dead too long and (b) the trauma hasn't been too bad. Exactly how the Probe works is complicated. As Professor Henry Steelman, the Probe's father, had said, "Let's just say it involves one part Incan shamanism and two parts cutting-edge technology." Steelman, alas, had always been widely regarded—in equal parts—as a brilliant scientist and a first-rank windbag. Sometimes the Probe worked; sometimes it didn't.

Brackett wasn't having much luck.

He'd been sitting next to the corpse of Dirk St. Romaine for the past half hour, while three different crime squads sent data back to the 107th hovering in a parking orbit above Tumbleweed. This data would later be used in re-creating a three-dimensional holo that was the exact reproduction of the crime scene. Various kinds of scientific crime units could then examine the scene at their leisure, reconstructing it into a variety of scenarios and variables.

Meanwhile, Brackett sat on the edge of a very bloody bed with this black styluslike instrument pointed against Dirk St. Romaine's forehead.

And Dirk wasn't saying a word.

"Any luck?" Obo said.

Brackett frowned. "None."

"Want me to try?" Daily said. She smiled. "Or don't you remember the last time?"

Brackett grumbled something incoherent.

The last time the trio had used the Steelman Probe to good effect, it was Jennifer Daily who had been wielding the stylus.

The dead man was a Nebban VIII narcotics dealer who had overdosed on some of his own merchandise.

Brackett had put the Probe into effect and shouted at the guy for twenty minutes. Then Obo took over and told the guy some totally incoherent Tau tales that were meant to be morally instructive. And finally Jennifer had a go at it. The guy started talking immediately. His brain wasn't quite dead yet and the guy was only too happy to chat with a very pretty Terran lady.

Brackett shrugged. "Be my guest."

So Daily sat down in Brackett's place and picked up the stylus.

Brackett's first impression was that Daily was tapping out some kind of rhythm on the corpse's forehead. Dit-dot-dot-dit or something like that.

Then Daily leaned forward and said, "I was a big fan of your books, Dirk. I really was. So this is really a thrill for me, even if it has to be under these conditions." She looked up at Obo and rolled her eyes; she'd always considered Dirk St. Romaine to be one of the universe's leading twinkies.

"But not everybody liked your work, Dirk," Daily went on after turning back to the corpse again, resuming the rhythm against his forehead. "That's why you were killed. Can you help us find out who that was? Please, Dirk, it's very important."

As the three of them sat there listening to the roaring silence, some people from the lab team came in. Obo occasionally expressed resentment toward all the "gadget people," as he called them. While the lab team brought enough hardware and paraphernalia along to start a department store, Obo often relied only on his extraordinary eyesight and his knowledge of computers to pick up the technical details in a given crime scene. Unfortunately, the lab people rarely asked for help of any kind, and showed quick, sharp irritation whenever Obo offered it.

Brackett stared at the corpse.

"He sure is talking up a storm," Brackett said.

"We haven't given him a chance yet," Daily said.

"No need to be defensive."

"I'm not defensive. Not at all."

Then she turned back to the dead guy and slapped him hard across the cheek. "Now, c'mon, Dirk, let's get down to serious business here. Tell me who the killer was."

Brackett and Obo looked at each other and smiled.

No, Daily wasn't getting defensive at all. That's why she'd belted the guy.

Brackett drifted out into the other room, where two resort cops were questioning a small, pale man in a dark business suit. He looked like a cartoon funeral director, right down to the rimless glasses and nervous mannerisms. The resort cops loomed over him, half shouting their questions. When one of them saw Brackett, he stopped shouting and signaled for Brackett to come over.

"Lieutenant Brackett, this is Matthew Pendrake. He was St. Romaine's private secretary."

Just before the two men shook hands, Brackett noticed Obo rushing out of the room. He wondered why the big Tau was going in such a hurry.

Brackett turned to Pendrake and said, "I'm sorry about all this, Mr. Pendrake."

"Poor Dirk. He was always afraid something like this would happen."

"He was?"

Pendrake nodded his small, blond head. "A lot of people hated him for telling the truth."

Brackett decided not to share his opinion of St. Romaine, that he'd been a vulture and the worst kind of pornographer, the kind who hurt other people.

"When did you see him last, Mr. Pendrake?"

"Last night."

"Did he seem frightened or nervous?"

"No, he was just sitting over there working."

"Wasn't he here on vacation?"

Pendrake sighed. It was a very dramatic sigh. "Dirk St. Romaine didn't know the meaning of vacation. And a motif planet is prime hunting grounds, anyway."

"Meaning what, exactly?"

"Well, there are a lot of celebrities here. Lots of drinking and drugging. Which means loose tongues. Which means Dirk spent a lot of time entering notes—you know, gossip, scuttlebutt, hearsay—into his computer."

"And that's what he was doing last night?"

"As far as I could tell. I stopped by here to see if he wanted to have some dinner but he was too busy at the computer."

"You didn't see what he was working on?" Brackett asked.

Pendrake laughed. It was a soft, friendly sound, the laugh of a small boy. "Dirk wouldn't let anybody near his screen when he was working. He was afraid you might figure out what he was up to. 'Knowledge is power,' he always said, and he meant it. And he didn't want to share his knowledge with anybody."

"Do you have any idea of what he might have learned while he was on Tumbleweed?"

Pendrake shook his head. "I handled his business affairs, bookings for vid shows, autographings, personal appearances, things like that. The books themselves . . . as I said, Dirk didn't believe in sharing."

The questions were too easy. He wanted to shake

up Mr. Pendrake here. "Were you aware that your employer was a blackmailer?"

Pendrake responded glibly. If Brackett had rattled him, he sure didn't show it. "Dirk was many things."

"Did he ever mention Wade Foster?"

"Of course. Everybody in the business knew he was going to write about Foster."

"Did people in the business have any idea exactly what he was going to write about Foster?"

Pendrake smiled sadly. "We're back to Dirk's personal affairs again, Lieutenant Brackett. He saw me strictly as an eminently expendable functionary."

"He sounds like a nice guy."

"That's about the only thing nobody ever accused him of."

"What's that?" Brackett said.

"Being a nice guy."

Brackett was just starting to smile, just starting to like this faded little man, when Jennifer screamed from the bedroom.

"My God," Pendrake said, paler than ever. "What was that?"

"You stay here. I'll go find out."

And with that, he drew his weapon and set off for the bedroom.

Chapter Five

Obo enjoyed tailing people. He was a big fan of private-eye vids and he figured any endeavor good enough for the likes of Robert Mitchum, Humphrey Bogart, and George Sanders as The Saint (his special favorite) was good enough for a Tau attached to a precinct station.

He had no idea whom he was tailing, just a somewhat swarthy, sinister Terran got up in a costume that seemed to be out of *The Arabian Nights*, what with a turban, a flowing white robe cinched at the waist, and a scabbard that bore a fearsome scimitar. The man had black eyes, a greasy little black beard and mustache, and a wart the size of Obo's thumbnail riding his right cheek.

Obo had first spotted him back at St. Romaine's cabin. While the boys and girls from the 107th had been conducting their investigation, the Arabian nights guy had walked past the open door at least six times. Obo knew immediately that this had been more than idle curiosity, and so he bolted the cabin and started following the man.

One thing was for sure, the guy had an appreciation for beauty.

He had spent the last fifteen minutes sauntering past the swimming pool; the grassy slope, where the ladies tanned themselves; and the outdoor restaurants, where the women sat in bikinis sipping sparkling summery drinks.

It was not until the man reached the escalator

angling down to all the expensive shops below that
Obo knew the man was on to him.

The man reached the escalator, turned around
suddenly and looked at Obo, and then took off running down the escalator steps, knocking people out of
his way as he went.

Obo considered that the long way down.

He ran over to the escalator, leaped up on the side
rail, and started running downward until he was in a
position to throw himself at the man.

Obo gave a mighty jungle call—another manner-
ism he'd picked up from vids, especially the ancient
Tarzan vids—and landed on the man with all the
force of his massive body.

The man went *ooomphf*, or something very much
like it, and sprawled all over the parquet floor of the
downstairs shopping mall.

Dozens of curious onlookers gathered, whispering,
pointing, smiling, shuddering. Tumbleweed was a
planet filled with violence but most of it was fake.
This had the sound and stink of the real thing, and
the real thing was always disturbing to see.

Obo knew he was getting appreciative looks from
some of the ladies.

A big, strapping Tau in a white cowboy suit was
just bound to win a few hearts.

He jerked the man to his feet and then pushed him
into the wall. Then he got his 107th badge out and
flashed it in front of the man's face.

"A lousy cop," the man said. Somehow, with his
turban and scimitar and his little pointed slippers,
the man should have said something with more of an
Arabic flavor.

"You seemed very interested in St. Romaine's
cabin."

"I'm just a nosy tourist," the man said, trying to
catch his breath. But his dark eyes were elusive.

"Name."

"Ahmed, the Master Mentalist."

"Real name, and make it snappy."

"Frank Boyle."

"Why are you on Tumbleweed?"

"I'm performing in one of the bistros tonight."

"Which one?"

"The Tumbling Tumbleweed."

"What's a mentalist?"

"I read minds. That sort of thing."

"You're saying you're a telepath?"

Frank Boyle smirked, seeming to imply that this big Tau here might just have been a hick. Everybody knew that there were only a handful of telepaths in the Federation, and nearly all of them had been bred in a special experiment long ago on a world called Xenon. Most of them, overwhelmed by their powers, had either killed themselves or been confined to institutions.

"I'm hardly a telepath, copper. I'm a failed actor trying to turn a credit or two and so I took up the ancient and dishonorable art of mind reading."

"Why all the interest in St. Romaine?"

"I'm just like everybody else. I enjoy a good juicy murder story."

Obo took another look at the man. The dark eyes were still elusive. The cruel mouth still hinted of a smirk. Obo wanted to take him in for further questioning but he knew just what Daily would say: "On what basis? What law has he violated? Just because he's sarcastic doesn't mean he's a criminal."

"The Tumbling Tumbleweed?"

Frank Boyle nodded. "Come early. There's a floor show before. A woman from your own world will be there." He winked. "Take my word for it, she's really something."

With that, Obo put his badge away.

Frank Boyle offered Obo a tiny, theatrical salute

and then ambled away toward the still-thrilled onlookers.

Obo still wanted to arrest him.

He didn't like guys who wore turbans and smirks.

When Brackett responded to Jennifer Daily's
scream, he wasn't sure what he was going to find in
the bedroom. It might be anything from a monster to
a second body hidden under the bed.

It was neither.

It was a pretty young woman, to whom Daily was
saying, sternly, "Sneaking in through a window that
way could get you killed sometime."

"Who's she?" Brackett said.

She was young, younger than Daily, and pretty in
a sad, almost wasted way. She wore a tan jumper,
which appeared to be grease stained. Her dark hair
was wild, as if she had not washed or combed it in
several days.

"How could he do this to me?"

"Who do what to you?" Daily said. She glanced at
Brackett, indicating she had the situation under control.

"Him. That creep St. Romaine."

"What did he do to you?"

"Promised me all kinds of money for some holos of
my boss in a compromising position—and then he
went and got himself murdered."

"Life's unfair when you come right down to it,"
Brackett said, rolling his eyes and writing the girl off
as a fetching lunatic.

The girl appeared to be coming out of a trance.
"Am I going to get arrested?"

Brackett said, "First, I want to know who you are
and how you got in here."

Daily supplied both answers. "Marcia Tenhold is
her name and she climbed through the bedroom window over there."

"How'd you know he was dead?" Brackett said.

"Everybody's talking about it," the girl said.

Brackett supposed that was true. "So your first reaction was to climb through a window into a murder
scene."

"I—I guess I sort of lost my mind."

"I wouldn't argue with that."

"I was just so furious. You don't know what it's like
working for Larry Bowman."

"Who?"

"Larry Bowman—the boxing champion."

"Oh right," Daily said. She didn't care for boxing
and in college had even protested to have it banned,
and so the Bowman name was unknown to her.

"If it's so bad, why don't you quit?" Daily said.

"Because if I quit, he'd fire my brother." She shook
her small, dark-haired head. She reminded Brackett
of a kitten. "The only way I can get freedom for either of us is to get enough money to buy out our con-
tract."

"And that's what St. Romaine offered you?"

"Yes."

"You have any idea where Bowman's been the past
six hours?"

She seemed thrilled at the implications of
Brackett's words. "You think he might be the killer?"

"So you don't know where he was?"

She shook her head. "I guess not."

Daily said, "Do you plan to bring charges?"

Brackett shook his head.

Daily said, "You got off easy. Next time, think before you act."

"That's what my mother always tells me."

"She's a sensible woman," Daily said.

"I'm sorry," the girl said, and looked as if she were
about to cry.

"Why don't you take her for a walk, Daily,"

Brackett said. He didn't need anybody crying in here. Things were crazy enough.

Daily nodded, and said, "I didn't get anywhere with St. Romaine. With the Steelman Probe and all."

"I didn't think you would. The trauma was too severe."

Daily took another look at the corpse and frowned. "He sure didn't seem to have many friends."

Brackett smiled. "Parasites rarely do, Daily, and that's just what St. Romaine was. A parasite."

"You're a very wise man, Lieutenant Brackett," Marcia Tenhold said. "I just wish more people had seen him that way."

Brackett nodded for Daily to get her out of here.

Daily took Marcia Tenhold gently by the shoulder and led her out of the room, and out of the cabin.

Chapter Six

Just as Daily was escorting the young girl away from the cabins, which were only a few minutes' walk from downtown with its casinos and fabulous shops, Obo was entering the lobby of Tumbleweed's largest hotel—the one where he and the other star cops just happened to be staying.

At any time of night or day, something was going on in the lobby. Now, for instance, a group of gypsy fiddlers stood tuning up while their agent was at the desk checking them into rooms. The fiddlers had their instruments tucked between jaw and shoulder and were giving a few curious customers a free home trial. Actually, they sounded pretty good.

Obo went right back to the manager's office.

"Howdy," said the blond behind the desk in the reception area at the back of the first floor.

Obo, remembering how Wade Foster did it on the vids, tipped his white ten-gallon hat and said, "Howdy yourself."

"May I help you?"

"I want a little information on one of your guests."

The young woman, all decked out in a fringe cowgirl costume, complete with a cute little hat that lay at a cute little angle on her cute little head, frowned mightily, as if he'd just suggested having sex in the lobby or something.

"Oh, we couldn't do that."

"Sure, we could."

"It's strictly against hotel rules."

Then Obo flashed his tin, wearing an expression he'd picked up from police vid shows.

"A star cop!" she said.

"Yes."

"Right here in our hotel!"

Out on the fringes, and especially on the motif worlds, one didn't often see star cops. Not many who identified themselves as such, anyway.

"Who were you inquiring about?" All gush and co-operation now.

"A Terran who calls himself Ahmed."

"The Master Mentalist?"

"That would be him."

"He's one of our star acts in the lounge."

"I'm sure he's a wonderful fellow. I'd just like access to your computer to learn a few more things about him."

She nodded. "See that room back there?"

"The blue door."

"Yes. That's where we keep access files on guests. I can give you the code."

"I'd appreciate it."

But she was back to fawning, forgetting the code momentarily. "You know, I never missed an episode of 'Star Cops, The Real Story.' "

Obo smiled. "You were a fan of that show, eh?"

"A big fan. I used to get weak kneed just watching all those cops running around in their tight gray uniforms."

When Taus were embarrassed, they didn't blush, but their right eye developed a tic.

"It was a bit exaggerated," Obo said, hoping to change the subject.

But the young woman persisted. "Are you going to be at the hotel tonight?"

"I imagine."

"How about going to see Ahmed's show with me?"

Obo tried to get used to how forward Terran

women were but he'd never quite adjusted yet. On
Tau Ceti, women had to be wooed with gifts even for
a casual stroll. He didn't like that process much, saw
it as demeaning to both men and women, but he did
appreciate, and find attractive, a certain reticence
among women of all species.

"All right," he said. After all, she was attractive.
"Now," he said, "how about that access code."

The young woman was positively beaming. "Of
course."

The last unit to enter the crime scene was the
psych probe. Their job was to do a profile on what
had gone on here, compare it to all the murders in
the computer, and see if there were any helpful simi-
larities. Murderers ran to types, and so did murders.
Ultimately, the psych-probe folks would pore over
police reports, autopsy and laboratory results,
sketches and photographs of the crime scene. This
was the unit that would construct the holographic
crime scene that investigators could walk into and
look around in, a scene based on the detailed workup
of the victim that included physical characteristics,
preferred clothing, sexual habits, likely response to
an approach by a stranger and reaction during an at-
tack. With all this data, the crime-probe folks could
reconstruct the sequence of events before, during,
and after the crime.

Brackett and Daily stood watching them work,
amazed and humbled as always. Brackett and Daily
were in the long and weary tradition of flatfoots.
There had been flatfoots in the ancient city of Athens
and in the teeming medieval cauldron of London and
the suicidal melting pot of twenty-first-century New
York. Flatfoots were nothing new, and nothing special. But the psych-probe folks . . . they were the true
unsung heroes of the 107th.

Morgan, the chief of psych probe, came out to the living room to talk to Brackett and Daily.

"You get anything on the Steelman?"

Brackett shook his head. "Nothing. Daily tried, too. She's a lot better at it than I am."

"I didn't get anything, either," Daily said.

"That's sure as hell a mess in there," Morgan said.

"I just wonder what the killer plans to do with the ears and eyes and hands."

"We've run into an awful lot of cannibalism lately," Morgan said, stuffing his hands deep into his white medical smock. None of the tech teams ever allowed themselves to get caught up in the given spirit of a motif world. They didn't, for example, don knightly attire on Lochinvar II, or wrap themselves in mastodon skin on TyRex II, nor did they dress up like town marshals on Tumbleweed. Obviously, as scientists, they saw all this costume-party nonsense as vaguely silly, and whenever they were around Brackett and looking at him got up in his kilts or leather jerkin or whatever the hell the planet called for, Brackett felt vaguely silly, too.

"You really think he'd eat them?" Daily said.

Morgan nodded to the room, his thinning gray hair revealing a pink, healthy scalp. He was just about to say something when his assistant Carver came through the door. Carver's nickname among the star cops was "Dracula" and for reasons that were obvious.

"God, Carver, what the hell have you been doing?" Morgan said.

Carver, his white medical smock streaked with blood and his hands soaked and lurid with the stuff, said, "Just checking things out, the way you told me."

Nepotism was not unknown on the 107th. Carver was the nephew of somebody powerful back at home base, and thus had been inflicted on the undeserving folks at the 107th. He was big, dumb, shaggy, and he seemed to revel in blood.

"Go wash up," Morgan said.

Carver looked sadly at his hands, as if he'd had no plans whatsoever of cleaning them. "All right, Chief," he said morosely, and walked over to the bathroom.

Which was when Daily noticed his shoulder. "Carver."

"Yeah?"

"Hold still."

"Huh?"

"Just stand there a minute."

"Something wrong?"

Daily said, "Look at his shoulder."

Brackett walked over with her to Carver for a closer look. He saw what Daily meant. Scattered over the top of Carver's jacket was some kind of sparkling dust. Brackett had never seen anything like it. "Come here," he said to Morgan.

Morgan took a look, too.

"Any idea what it is?" Brackett said.

"Not really."

"How about you, Carver? You notice the sparkling stuff on your shoulder before this?"

"Huh-uh."

Daily touched a finger to the sparkling material. "It's hot."

"Hot?" Morgan said, leaning closer and touching it with his own finger. "Hot," he said. "I wonder what the hell it is."

"I don't feel good," Carver said.

"Where don't you feel good?" Brackett said.

"Sort of all over. Like I have the flu or something."

"I'll get you a room at the hotel. You can lie down there."

Carver nodded. And then collapsed.

"Hey!" several people seemed to shout at the same time as they piled toward Carver.

They got him up on the couch and loosened his shirt. Brackett got him water and Daily opened the windows.

They were just walking back to him, when the phone rang and one of the resort cops said, "Lieutenant Brackett, it's for you."

Brackett thanked him, went over, and took the phone.

"Brackett."

He recognized instantly the unfriendly voice of his unfriendly boss Captain Jason Carnes, a much-decorated Academy graduate who believed in the supremacy of such graduates.

"Yes."

"You can call off your investigation."

"What?"

"Just what I said. I'm afraid we weren't able to be much good." He paused. "I'm not holding you responsible, by the way."

"Captain, would you tell me what's going on?"

"You mean you haven't heard?"

"Heard what?"

"Wade Foster. The man we were sent to Tumbleweed to keep out of trouble."

"What about him?"

"He's in the manager's office at the hotel you're staying at and . . . and he's just confessed to the murder of Dirk St. Romaine."

"But . . ."

"I'll meet you at the hotel in an hour. I'm coming planetside in a few minutes."

"Yes, sir."

Brackett hung up and glanced over at Carver. Even from here, Brackett could see that the man was seriously ill.

What the hell was the strange, sparkling dust on his jacket?

And why the hell was Wade Foster, strong-jawed, blue-eyed hero of billions, confessing to the murder of a twit like Dirk St. Romaine?

Chapter Seven

Obo spent half an hour checking into the background of the man who called himself Ahmed, the Master Mentalist.

Somebody once estimated—proving that each person's existence has a purpose after all—that in the Federation worlds there are more than 73,000 cocktail lounges. This means that at any time in the Federation, more than, say, 5,000 performers are doing the same thing a long-ago performer named Wayne Newton did, trying with great and sweaty effort to conceal the fact that they have very little talent.

While Ahmed was not a singer, he was the next-worst thing, one of those intense little men who tried to convince his audience that he had magical powers: This included throwing a smoke bomb and saying abracadabra; pulling some poor scruffy little bunny out of a hat; or, most offensive of all, pretending to be reading minds. Okey-dokey, your royal Master Mentalistship. Ahmed exhibited intelligence on only one score. He was smart enough to bring on stage with him a creamy and voluptuous young woman named Shana, his stage assistant. The male part of the audience would therefore have its attention diverted from all of the Master Mentalist's hoary tricks. They'd be too busy eyeballing Shana to notice what a shabby little flimflam man Ahmed was.

But that wasn't the entire Master Mentalist story. As usual with these guys, the holos and data of their

backgrounds were accompanied by seemingly endless criminal records.

For example, when he was fifteen, Ahmed (né
Frank Boyle) broke into a home for the blind and began stealing everything he could stuff into a Santa
Claus bag. When he was twenty-five, the Master
Mentalist was the key player in a scam designed to
separate a dowager from her billions by pretending
to be in beyond-the-grave contact with her late husband, a slave owner and all-around Federation-class
asshole. True, this scam was at least as old as Midas
but sometimes the oldest scams were the best. The
star cops estimated that Ahmed had bilked the old
lady out of 6 million credits before they'd broken up
his little game. Finally, among the dozens of all other
charges, was the recent altercation the Master Mentalist had had with the one and only Shana. According to half a dozen eyewitnesses, he tried to push her
out of a fourteenth-story hotel window on Cykle IV,
where the duo had been performing their act in a
lounge elegantly named The Grin And Bare It.

So this was Ahmed, small-time entertainer, small-
time con man, and if the incident on Cykle IV was to
be believed, would-be murderer.

Why would such a man be walking back and forth
in front of Dirk St. Romaine's cabin after St. Romaine had been murdered?

Obviously, the Master Mentalist had an abiding
interest in the case, but what was it?

The alert cell in Obo's wristwatch sounded. Obo
froze the computer screen where it was at and
punched his wristwatch into alert II mode.

"Obo?"

"Right."

"Brackett."

"I probably should have told you where I was going. But I wanted to follow this guy."

"Tell me later. Right now we've got a real problem."

"What's that?"

"Wade Foster has confessed to killing St. Romaine."

Obo spoke one of his race's foulest words. Unfortunately, he'd never been able to translate it for any Terran. They just had to take his word for it that it was bad. *Really* bad.

"Exactly," Brackett said, as if he understood the word perfectly. "Captain Carnes is coming down here to meet us now."

"Bet he's happy."

"Delirious," Brackett said. "So why don't you get over here now, too. We may need you."

"Be there momentarily, Lieutenant," Obo said, switching alert off, and then looking back at the monitor.

There was probably a lot more to learn about the Master Mentalist but there wasn't time for that now.

Obo switched off the unit, clipped off the light sensors in the room, and went out to the desk where the blond in the fringe cowboy costume sat.

"You must really have been working!" she said. "You were in there for more than a half hour."

"Thanks for letting me use your computer. Less hassle for me than calling up to the ship."

Obo started walking out toward the lobby.

"Don't forget our date tonight," the blond called.

"Impossible. I'm looking forward to it."

The blond cooed, and then went back to work.

There was a rumor—many rumors—that the men and women working in the lab of any given precinct ship believed that they were a cut above (well, *several* cuts above) all the other people aboard.

Well, maybe it was a little bit true, but who wouldn't have a swelled head if his or her department solved something like 60 percent of the crimes investigated in a year's time.

True facts. The lab on any given precinct ship was perhaps the most valuable amount of floor space aboard. While the star cops were out alternately playing Sherlock Holmes, Mike Hammer, V.I. Warshawski, and a blue Tau investigator named Uku (Obo's role model), the boys and girls in the lab (or so their version goes) were doing the real work.

Leave the fistfights, the tailing, the electronic eavesdropping to the star cops—and let the lab folks have a go at blood, hair, fingerprints, and fibers discovered at a crime scene. With this sort of information, the crime lab people could not only tell who did it but when it happened and how it happened, which was exactly the kind of information needed in a Federation court to get a conviction. Hard, solid evidence. Not intuition. Not conjecture. Not a flashy and beguiling "possibly true" scenario. But hard evidence. "Just the facts, ma'am," as Detective Sergeant Joe Friday always liked to say.

So it was, approximately an hour after the discovery of Dirk St. Romaine's body, that the crime lab aboard precinct ship 107 went to work on seventy-two different pieces of information to be analyzed and assessed, among them a curious sparkling dust that had sent a young cop named Carver to the hospital.

The man in charge at the moment was named John Paul Johansen, a stolid blond scientist given to white medical coats (most lab people just wore the regular star cop uniform) and sucking on an ancient gnarly pipe that had once belonged to an ancient ancestor of his.

Lieutenant Johansen was at the receiving module when the data began arriving, his eight other lab folks already busy with other cases. (This precinct ship worked on cases for more than one hundred inhabited worlds at any given time, so it was frequently, as now, overloaded with work.)

As Johansen watched the screen, the computers already classifying all material and information by category, he saw the first mention of the sparkling dust.

And he smiled. A great big blond smile it was, too, because this was just the sort of thing a lab person is eager to find.

There were burglaries and there were murders and there were sabotages, and to the average person, they all might seem pretty romantic. But actually they were pretty dull, because all their elements—at least from the lab's point of view—were the same thing over and over. Do up a holo of the crime scene. Write a DNA "biography" of the perpetrator (or "perp," as lab folks liked to say). Identify the perp in the suspect computer.

But a mysterious sparkling space dust that was hot to the touch and had made at least one star cop so sick he had to be taken to the hospital (nothing personal, you understand)? This was the kind of thing people like John Paul Johansen begged for, prayed for.

With something like mysterious space dust (a) your colleagues would immediately be envious, (b) your next chance for promotion just took a big leap forward, and (c) you stood a good chance of winning a Moskowitz, one of the esteemed forensic awards (named for the corps's first forensic scientist, Frank Moskowitz) given out annually.

Sitting at his computer station, Johansen looked furtively around, trying to see if any of the others were taking note of his unalloyed glee.

They weren't.

And so it was, knowing he was going to work right through dinnertime and well into a second and third shift if necessary, so it was that John Paul Johansen with his silly little affected pipe and his big blond grin, got to work on trying to figure out just exactly what this sparkling mysterious space-dust crap was anyway.

He could see himself clutching his Moskowitz now.

On his way down in the shuttle craft, Captain Jason Carnes was thinking of all the ways Wade Foster's confession would damage the corps.

Over the past ten years, the corps had suffered from an increasingly bad image, thanks to some of the frontier cops—i.e., those who operated in one- or two-person scout ships, not on a precinct ship, and who, along with their chores as cops, hired out as thieves, thugs, and, in a few instances, killers.

Now a whole new generation of TV kiddies were about to be told that their favorite guy, "Saddle Pard" himself, whom they associated with the "proud-tradition star cops," had killed some little twit of an author because said little twit of an author was blackmailing him.

Oh, yeah, just what the force needed.

And a particular blow to a man like Carnes, whose family went back six generations on the force.

Carnes looked at his reflection in the curve of the cockpit window. He was a small man, with slicked-down black hair, eyebrows so black and thick they almost looked fake, and a potbelly he kept trying to hide inside his natty captain's coat, the one with all the fancy gold buttons.

Dreesen said, "Sir?"

Carnes brought his waning attention back to the ship and looked at the handsome young man piloting the small craft. David Dreesen was an inquisitor, a man skilled both in psychology and law. He did all the interrogating for the 107th. Many prisoners that nobody else had been able to crack snapped quickly under Dreesen's relentless questioning. Maybe it was his farm-boy looks, the blond crew cut, the friendly blue eyes, the respectful way he had with men, and the downright courtly way he had with women.

"Yes?" Carnes said.

"You said there was something you wanted to talk to me about."

"Yes, Dreesen, there is."

Carnes swung around in his copilot's seat. With his burgeoning belly, these small craft were starting to be a tight fit.

Carnes started to say something and then stopped himself. He always hated this part of the job. This sort of thing was really none of his business, but as captain of the 107th, he had to make sure that people got along. And romance was one way to make sure that people *didn't* get along.

"You and Jennifer are friends."

"Yes, sir."

Carnes noticed instantly how the young man tensed up. Blood rose in his neck, spread upward to his cheeks.

"Very good friends, I might say."

"Yes, sir, I guess you could say that."

Staring straight ahead; not looking at Carnes at all.

"But last night when I was making my final rounds for the evening, I was walking past the corridor leading to Daily's cabin and I saw—"

Dreesen's shoulders slumped. He looked as if he had just been punched in the solar plexus by an invisible fist. "You saw Jennifer slap me."

"Yes; yes, I did."

"Very hard."

"And right across the face," Carnes said.

"It's because she loves me, sir."

"I see. I guess times have changed then."

"Sir?"

"Well, in the old days, when a young woman

slapped a young man like that, it usually meant she was angry with him."

"Yes, sir."

"But these days, at least according to what you just told me, it means she loves him."

"Yes, sir."

"What the hell was going on there last night, Dreesen?"

"Sir?"

"Why the hell did Jennifer slap you?"

"I told you. Because she loves me so much she's frustrated and—"

The blush was back. It filled his face.

"Sir?"

"Yes."

"Is it really necessary that we continue having this conversation?"

"I suppose not. But I don't want to see Daily slap you again."

"No, sir."

"That's impermissible conduct aboard ship."

"Yes, sir."

"And I want you to tell her that for me."

"Yes, sir. It was really my fault anyway."

"I don't give a damn whose fault it was, Dreesen. I just don't want it to happen again."

"Yes, sir."

But Carnes had already forgotten about romance and was already thinking of the trouble with Wade Foster.

"This is going to be a disaster; a goddamn disaster," Carnes said.

"Yes, sir."

"A goddamned disaster."

"Yes, sir," Dreesen said miserably. He still *was* thinking about romance. "Yes, sir."

Chapter Eight

All over the gambling section of the city, vacationers in various kinds of spangly Western clothes stood craning their necks up at huge vid screens that carried stories of the unthinkable: Wade Foster, the same smiling galoot their kids had trusted for years, had admitted to committing a murder.

Inside the hotel, the entire second floor had been cordoned off. Casino guards stood at attention, looking eager to open fire.

Inside the cordon, inside a large party room, ten star cops stood looking at a man in the center of the room.

The man sat in a chair. He wore a blue Western shirt with white piping and white pearl buttons; blue Western trousers with white piping; and modified Texas boots (he had fat toes, and so the boots weren't quite so narrow in the toes) that had his initials, WF, carved in leather across the arch. This was, of course, Wade Foster.

When Foster looked up at Brackett, all the cop could think of was himself on the day he'd found his wife murdered. Disbelief had given way to disorientation—an inability, at least temporarily, to face what had happened here. That's how Foster looked now. Brackett felt sorry for him.

"May I have a glass of water?"

Captain Carnes nodded for a glass of water to be brought to the man.

Foster drank in gulps. Some of the wet, silver stuff

trickled down his chin. It was easy to see how badly his right hand was shaking.

Just as Foster was finishing his water, Obo came through the rear door and leaned against the wall, watching the vid star make his confession. While he watched, he softly whistled, "I'm A Fightin' Buckaroo, I Am, I Am." He couldn't get the tune from his mind and it was driving him crazy.

The star cops had been in this room for three hours now. Dreesen, the interrogator, had asked him relentless questions for a relentless hour. For once, Dreesen wasn't trying to get somebody to confess. He was simply trying to make Foster's story make sense.

"You say you went over to St. Romaine's cabin?" Dreesen had asked.

"Yes."

"What time was this?"

"I'm not sure."

"Take a guess."

"Maybe two A.M."

"You said that before, so we checked with your valet. He was up at that time and he swears you were in bed sleeping."

"He's being loyal."

"What was St. Romaine doing when you got there?"

"Uh, drinking and watching the vid."

"You're sure of that?"

"Yes."

"The contents of Mr. St. Romaine's stomach have been analyzed. There was no alcohol in his system."

"I didn't say he was drinking alcohol."

"Then what do you think he was drinking?"

"Just something in a glass. It could have been anything."

"So you went inside?"

"Yes."

"Mr. St. Romaine's cabin had a double security system. How did you get in?"

"I walked in."

"Through the security system?"

"I knocked and told him I wanted to see him."

"So you went inside and talked?"

"Yes."

"For how long?"

"I'm . . . uh . . . not sure."

"What did you talk about?"

"I told him I was willing to pay what he'd been asking for that material about me."

"In other words, you were giving in to blackmail?"

"Yes."

"So you were prepared to pay him what he was asking?"

"Yes."

"Had you brought enough money with you?"

"Yes. I wanted to get it over with."

"You're not making sense, Mr. Foster."

"What?"

"Your story doesn't make any sense. If you'd brought the money along to pay him, why did you kill him?"

Foster had stared up at Dreesen blankly.

"Did you hear me, Mr. Foster?"

"What?"

"I said that your story doesn't make any sense."

"I killed him. That I'm sure of, I was drunk and I just don't remember things clearly."

"Even though you were going to pay him the money, you killed him?"

"Yes."

"Why did you kill him?"

The blank stare had come again. "I'm tired," Foster had said. "I just want to sit here now."

This was half an hour ago.

Foster still sat in the uncomfortable chair the hotel manager had provided. Foster's eyes still looked blank, confused.

Foster handed the empty glass back to a cop and then wiped the water from his chin.

Captain Carnes was going over the preliminary reports with Brackett. Even though Carnes didn't care for the man personally, he did respect his abilities.

Carnes was flipping the page to the report sent to the crime lab when Dreesen came over and said, "He's lying."

Carnes and Brackett looked up immediately. "What?" Carnes said.

"He's lying. I don't think he killed St. Romaine."

"But he seems to think so."

"Yes. Maybe he's psychotic. Maybe he hated St. Romaine so much that he just started *thinking* he killed him."

"He's already told the media," Carnes said. "And those bastards have already put the story all over the Federation."

Dreesen sighed. "We probably can't prove he didn't do it, anyway."

"We can't?"

"No. I mean, he seems to know all the basics. How St. Romaine was killed—the eyes and hands and ears and so forth—roughly when he was killed. If he wants to stick to his story, we'll have a hard time disproving it."

Brackett looked at Carnes. "Mind if I talk to him?"

"Be my guest."

Carnes and Dreesen watched as Brackett went over to the man.

"Hello, Mr. Foster."

Eyes staring upward. Blankly. "I killed him." Drool running silver down the left side of his mouth.

"Would you do something for me, Mr. Foster?"

"What's that?"

"Eat a piece of candy."

"Pardon me?"

"Eat a piece of candy."

"Why?"

"Just a little experiment."

"Are you trying to trick me into something?"

"No, I'm not, Mr. Foster."

Carnes leaned into Dreesen and whispered, "What the hell's he trying to do?"

And Dreesen whispered back, "I don't know but whatever it is, it's interesting."

From the slash pocket of his trousers, Brackett took a small piece of candy gaily wrapped in crinkly mauve-colored paper.

Ahmed, the Master Mentalist, could not have looked more magical than Brackett did at the moment as he held the small piece of candy between thumb and forefinger.

"See this, Mr. Foster?"

"Uh-huh."

"It's candy."

"Candy."

"Right. Candy. Do you have a sweet tooth?"

"Uh-huh."

"Good. Then you like candy?"

"I still don't understand what you're doing."

"Just trust me, Mr. Foster. Now, because we're recording all this, I want you to tell me if you like candy or not."

"I like candy."

"Would you say that a little louder?"

"I like candy."

"Fine. Then, here, why don't you take this?"

Wade Foster stared dumbly at the mauve-wrapped candy.

"No, thanks."

"What?"

"I said no, thanks. I guess I don't feel like eating candy right now."

Carnes stepped forward and said, "Brackett, just what the hell are you doing? I don't blame him for not wanting any candy at a time like this. I wouldn't, either."

"Just give me a few more minutes here, sir, all right?"

Brackett turned back to Wade Foster. "I'm just trying to help you, sir."

Foster seemed increasingly despondent. "I appreciate that."

"Then will you at least give this candy a try?"

He shrugged. "I guess."

He put out his hand, palm up.

Brackett dropped the candy in it.

"Give it a try, Mr. Foster."

Foster smiled bleakly up at Carnes. "You've got a very persistent officer here."

"Persistent isn't the only thing he is," Carnes said.

Foster gaped down at the mauve-wrapped candy. "It's funny. Like I said, I've usually got a sweet tooth."

"Unwrap it, Mr. Foster."

Foster obliged Brackett and unwrapped it.

A small piece of butterscotch rested in his palm.

"Pick it up, Mr. Foster."

Again, almost robotically, Foster complied.

He held the candy between thumb and forefinger, as if this were some kind of triumphant moment. "It's candy, all right."

"Put it in your mouth now, if you would, Mr. Foster."

Another bleak Foster smile, again aimed at Carnes. "He never gives up, does he?"

Carnes glowered.

Foster put the candy in his mouth.

Closed his lips.

The candy sat in there one, two minutes.

Foster stared at Brackett and Carnes. Nothing

happened. He was just this big, sad guy sitting there in these fancy cowboy duds.

Carnes glared at Brackett, then turned to walk away.

And that's just when Foster let go.

An arcing stream of orange vomit gushed from his mouth, splashed all over the floor.

Hard to say which was more sickening, the sound or sight of the stuff.

Carnes wheeled around, sensing that some of the orange vomit had managed to taint his otherwise impeccably polished black boots.

He glared at Brackett again.

Despite the stench, Brackett was smiling.

"Since when are you a pharmacologist?" Carnes said, twenty minutes later.

"I don't claim to be a pharmacologist."

"You could have killed that man."

"I've seen the reaction before. I knew what would happen."

"You *thought* you knew what would happen, Brackett. But there was no guarantee that he'd react the way you thought he would."

The two men were in a room off the area they'd been using for interrogation. Carnes had specifically requested that he be alone with Brackett. The place was an anteroom that had apparently been used for a party. Little pink plastic glasses holding the remains of punch littered the long tables, along with crumpled napkins, cake crumbs, and plates with foul-looking stains on them.

Carnes took several deep breaths, calming himself down. "I want to thank you for helping me out there."

Brackett looked shocked at Carnes's cordial tone. He was used to the combative mode.

"But that still didn't give you any right to risk Foster's life."

Back in his criminal days, one of Brackett's accomplices had given a guard a drug that induced psychosis. They'd kept the man tied up for two days. Any time they tried to feed him food with sugar in it, he vomited violently. The guard had become so susceptible to thought control that he eventually opened up the vault for them, thinking—as they had suggested—that he was actually one of their accomplices.

Seeing how disoriented Wade Foster was, and sensing how unnaturally eager he was to confess to the murder, Brackett had started thinking about the guard and the drug they'd given him and the way he'd throw up whenever he was given any amount of sugar.

Brackett had decided to see if Foster had been given a similar drug.

"We're going to charge him?" Brackett said. "I mean, do you really think he did it?"

Carnes chose not to answer the question directly.

"We'll have to. Look at it this way. With the report of Foster's confession all over the Federation, if we say he was given a drug that convinced him he was the killer, a drug that tricked him into making a false confession—who'll believe us? Unless we have the real killer to hand, the media will scream 'cover-up' and say we're just trying to protect ourselves and our spokesman. We need the real killer." He shook his head, angry and miserable. "No, for now, we'll have to let his confession stand." He looked grimly at Brackett. "And in the meantime, you're going to have to find the killer. And fast."

He sighed. "The whole reputation of the force is at stake here, Brackett." He frowned. "I suppose you think I'm being sentimental, but being an academy graduate the force means a great deal to me. I don't want people thinking that our spokesperson—and a hero to billions of kids—is a murderer. We need to find the perp, Brackett, and right away."

"I'll do my best, Captain." For the first time in their six-year relationship, Brackett actually felt like saluting this chunky, pompous, sour little man. This was the first time Carnes had ever shown any regard whatsoever for Brackett.

Carnes returned the salute. "A lot of people are depending on you, Brackett."

Brackett nodded. "I'm aware of that, Captain."

And with that, he was gone, leaving Carnes to brood about the heritage and traditions of the force that the news networks so liked to savage.

Carnes smiled bitterly.

What ever happened to all those blond, blue-eyed, steel-jawed heroes of yesteryear, anyway?

Brackett sure wasn't Carnes's idea of a hero.

Chapter Nine

Daily made sure she left the interrogation room before Dreesen. She didn't want to see him.

She had just about reached the escalator when she heard him call her name.

Feigning deafness, Daily started walking down the moving stairs quickly.

Maybe if she reached the crowd on the mezzanine floor she could lose him. . . .

A hand took her shoulder. "Jennifer, I'd really like to talk to you."

She didn't look back at him. "I told you yesterday, I just want to be left alone."

"It's important, Jennifer. Just five minutes."

"No."

"There's a coffee shop right downstairs and—"

"No."

"Please, Jennifer. Please."

She knew she would give in. Damn.

In this part of the Federation, the servitude class consisted of Arcturans, who were all the things you get in such a class—clean, punctual, hardworking, and tirelessly surly. Several decades ago, the Arcturans had been warriors. They'd destroyed many planets and many species, including the Tekkan IVs, a poor doglike species that the Arcturans had virtually wiped out of existence. The Federation Council, nothing if not sly, had decided to punish the next three generations of Arcturans by turning them into waiters and waitresses. But after you'd been served by an Arcturan, you wondered who was punishing whom.

This waitress, nice enough looking, smacked her gum, openly picked her nose, and rolled her eyes when Daily had the audacity to linger a moment over the menu. The waitress was dressed up as—what else?—a cowgirl.

"You think I ain't got nothin' else to do?" the waitress said. "Jesus H. Christ in a bobsled."

Dreesen decided to be brave and try and stare the woman down but such an attempt was foolish. Nobody had steelier eyes than a waitress from Arcturus.

"Just coffee, I guess," Daily said.

"You coulda said that five minutes ago," the waitress said, violently <u>snatching</u> the menu from Daily's hands.

She flounced off, shaking her head and twitching her nice round hips for the sake of two space sailors sitting at the crowded counter. These boys, hicks far from their home world, were obviously in need of female companionship.

"I'm sorry about yesterday," Dreesen said.

"I didn't have any right to slap you. I'm sorry, too."

"I've just been pushing too hard."

"No, you're right to push. It's time I face my problem."

"It's not a problem."

"My dilemma, then."

"I really love you, Jennifer."

"I know you do."

"Do you love me?"

But the waitress was back. She slammed their coffees down, spilling brown steaming liquid over the table, all the while smacking her gum.

"Anything else I can getcha?"

"Nothing right now, thanks," Dreesen said.

"Just remember, nobody'll shoot you if you leave a good tip."

"I'll remember that."

"Yeah, I'll bet," the waitress said, and flounced away again.

Dreesen put out his hand and touched Daily's. "Captain Carnes asked me about you this morning. He saw you slap me."

"Oh, God," Daily said, her lovely cheeks tinting red. She felt like a high school girl, foolish and out of control. She was supposed to be an adult, for God's sake, serving on one of the most celebrated precinct ships in the entire force, the 107th.

And now here she was . . .

"What else did he say?"

"He just said we should, you know, conduct ourselves properly. And he reminded me how shipboard romances can mess things up professionally. And he—"

"He thinks I'm messing up my career."

"He didn't say that at all, Jennifer."

"Don't you see, David? We can't keep seeing each other. It will destroy our careers."

For the past six months, Dreesen had been asking her to marry him. But she was worried about the impact of such a union on both their careers. She'd seen other couples drift into marriage and invariably their careers lost momentum. For Jennifer, being a star cop was everything she'd imagined it would be. And she didn't want to stop. She wanted to rise quickly in the ranks.

"Jennifer, it doesn't have to destroy our careers."

"I've seen other couples and it—"

"Well, it may affect other couples that way but that doesn't mean it'll happen to us."

"I need time, David—time to think."

"But you've been saying that for the past six

months. The same old thing and—" He caught himself and looked embarrassed. "I'm sorry."

"There's nothing to be sorry about."

"Sure, there is. I'm whining again. God, I hate that tone that comes into my voice."

She looked over at him and smiled. She really liked his face, but in that moment she realized she didn't *love* his face, and when she realized that, she knew that she didn't love him, either. Oh, he was nice and reliable, and certainly dutiful as a lover, but somehow . . .

But God, how could she ever tell him?

"I love you, Jennifer."

And then she saw the silver tears glisten in his blue eyes. He was so damned *nice*. Why couldn't he be a jerk like many of the men she dated? Jerks were easy to deal with. But Dreesen was like holding this sad little Christmas puppy up to your face and telling him that you had to put him to sleep. The big sleep.

"I just need more time."

He smiled a sad, broken smile. "Then that's what you'll have, Jennifer, because I love you. Time."

She dropped her eyes.

They sat for a time in silence.

Then, "David?"

"If we keep going out—"

"*If* we keep going out—God, Jennifer, why *wouldn't* we keep going out?"

"All right, *when* we go out, then . . ."

"Yes?"

"I don't want to talk about it."

"About what?"

She dropped her eyes again.

"About any of it, David. About love or marriage or—anything."

It was as if she had just wounded him in some fatal

way. She could see that but what could she do about
it?

Didn't she have the right to be honest?

"Just when we go out, David, let's . . . let's just
have a nice time. There are so many things to do on
the ship, fun things. We don't have to sit around and
be serious all the time, do we?"

He could barely speak. "I suppose not."

"We'll just have good times, the way we did in the
beginning, the way . . ."

Now, David let his attention roam across the coffee
shop. He looked on the verge of tears.

"Brackett's holding a briefing, David. I'm sorry
but I've got to go."

His eyes, sad and just beginning to reflect anger,
met hers.

"I know you love me, Jennifer. I know you do."

My God, why was she still a virgin at twenty-
eight?

He would have said more but the waitress came
over and glared down at the table.

"See that?" she said to Dreesen.

"See what?" he said, sounding annoyed.

"That empty space where the tip should be."

"Oh."

He nervously brought change from his pocket and
dropped it on the table.

"Gee," the waitress said, "I hope that doesn't
bankrupt you or anything."

As Dreesen finished settling the bill, Jennifer
mouthed a silent good-bye and rushed from the coffee shop.

The waitress said, "Looks like you two got a little
problem, huh?"

Then she took her tip and her sensitivity and went
away.

Dreesen fled the coffee shop, trying to catch up
with Jennifer.

This time he didn't have any luck.
She was gone.

Brackett, Obo, and a half dozen other star cops
were watching a vid when Daily arrived for the briefing.

The vid's subject was none other than a parasite
named Dirk St. Romaine.

Daily took a seat in the dark room and watched
along with her fellow cops.

*Dirk St. Romaine is born William Bunkley in a
small Ohio river town. His father is a leading mem-
ber of the local neo-fascist movement and young William is only too happy to help out, particularly in
pillaging synagogues and splashing animal blood all
over the interior. Anti-Semitism (among many other
antis) is fashionable again and so young William
finds a great deal of support for his activities. Unfortunately, neither neo-fascism nor anti-Semitism pays
especially well, so young William goes on to the state
university, where he and some other like-minded
youngsters manage to take over the student newspa-
per and inflict on the students a fascist's view of political correctness (to be fair, the left-wing students have
been inflicting their addle-brained version of political correctness on the student body for decades). After
graduation, it is on to Gotham, where young William
spends an obscure decade working for at least a
dozen shrill but empty magazines that go out of business as quickly as fireflies on a summer night. But
then, ah, but then, our story turns: the screen shows
some home vid of a thirty-year-old Bunkley arguing
with a famous Broadway actress outside a famous
Broadway pub. (A) Bunkley's date for the evening, a
struggling film director of the tortured artiste school,
just happens to have her camera along and (B) inside
the pub, Bunkley has just happened to insult the actress's date, who is of the extremely languid haute*

couture *crowd. Their argument spills onto the pavement. It makes for great video, especially the part
where the actress slaps Bunkley across the mouth.
Then she and her mate flounce off to their waiting
limo.*

*That night, lying in the darkness of his obscure
bed, Bunkley begins to develop the idea that will eventually make him rich and famous. What if an unknown young man (him) were to research and write
an article on the famous actress (her) who had just
slapped (him) across the mouth?*

*There is only one way Bunkley can repay the bitch
for her slap. He spends the next six weeks following
her, going through her garbage, talking to every en-
emy she's made on the concrete isle (a formidable
number), and then taking everything he's learned
and turning it into an article titled, "Growing Old
Gracelessly." Knowing that his real name has no
magic, he signs the piece "Dirk St. Romaine" and dispatches the article to a number of tabloids. None
takes it. Sure, the woman is a bitch, no doubt about it,
but she is a powerful bitch and even the tabs tremble
at her power. Fortunately, for our boy and our story,
there resides in Gotham a guy named LeFevre, who
has his own half-hour talk show on one of the public-
access porno channels (he frequently spends the entire half hour sitting nude on a plastic beanbag
chair), discussing whatever is on his mind. Well,
LeFevre has a friend at one of the tabs (no surprise, is
it?) who gives him a copy of Dirk St. Romaine's vile
piece on the vile actress, and LeFevre (no literary
critic) is so impressed he reads it on his show. The
piece is so nasty, so mean, and so pathetically funny
that the public-access channel is inundated with
calls to run it again. And again. And again. The piece
becomes the talk of Gotham. The actress threatens
to sue, of course, and various injunctions are got
against both Dirk St. Romaine and LeFevre (who was*

*at last a genuine star). But they keep on running the
piece anyway.*

And St. Romaine's career starts to build.

*Soon after this, a major publisher calls St. Ro-
maine, tells him to choose a subject, and they'll give
him not only lots of cash but a whole slew of private
investigators and together they can set out to destroy
anybody they choose. St. Romaine is thrilled. Not
even neo-fascism had been this much fun.*

*Thus is the glitzy career of Dirk St. Romaine
launched to great and lurid fanfare.*

The vid now skips seven years.

*St. Romaine is the most hated writer on the planet.
Maybe in the entire Federation. He has brought down
at least six careers. Decimated them. Two of the people killed themselves. (St. Romaine expressed no re-
morse. "I tell the truth and let the chips fall where
they may." One wag said yes, cow chips.)*

*In addition to being the most hated writer on the
planet, he is also the richest and most popular. He is
mobbed the way rock stars are mobbed; he is envied
the way movie stars are envied. He has bedded the
most beautiful women of his time (they're afraid to
say no) and he has humbled the most arrogant of
men.*

*Then he writes the Smythe book, Smythe being
earth's ambassador to the Federation League, the
most important political body among all the worlds.
Smythe is in his sixties, a white-haired, venerable
statesman and intellectual revered by all three major
political parties, and owned by none.*

*Certain stories are whispered to Dirk St. Romaine.
Stories about Andrew Smythe's sexual preferences.
Vile stuff.*

*Just the sort of thing to set young William
Bunkley's brain aflutter.*

*Heretofore, Dirk St. Romaine had written only
about entertainment figures.*

*A book about the planet's most revered political fig-
ure will not only win St. Romaine new readers, it may
even win him (at last) some begrudging respect from
the newsies.*

*So he spends a year and a half writing his book,
said tome being kept completely secret except to his
editor and publisher. They are nervous but exultant.*

The book appears.

*And on the day the book appears, a mysterious let-
ter is faxed to St. Romaine's publisher.*

A HOAX, YOU STUPID ASSHOLE. I FED ST. ROMAINE HOURS
OF FALSE INFORMATION ABOUT SMYTHE. HOPE YOU AND
DIRKIE-POO ENJOY ALL THE LITIGATION.

And my God, is there litigation.

Everybody sues.

*Sometimes it seems that even some of Smythe's
long-deceased blood kin are suing.*

*The publisher is destroyed, and ends up working
for a magazine for car buffs.*

Smythe is more than ever the hero.

And St. Romaine is . . . gone.

Nobody knows where.

*The vid spent five minutes speculating on all the
possibilities. He is said to be in South America, he is
said to be on Deneb IV, he is said to be dead by his
own hand in a sleazy Bombay hotel room.*

*For seven years, nobody hears from him. Not that
anybody is particularly sorry about this.*

*Then he resurfaces, gets a deal with a small pub-
lisher to do a job on a popular vid actress, and the
book is published.*

*Nobody in publishing has ever read anything like
this.*

It is the most intimate *biography published. It
claims to know things about her that she wouldn't tell
anybody, not even her closest friend.*

*The actress sues, of course, but it is a useless suit.
The industry knows that this is not another Smythe.
St. Romaine has managed to learn the real (and
sleazy and sad) truth about the ravishing actress who
was once a man.*

*And St. Romaine is once again publishing's least
respected but most successful author.*

*He publishes five books in as many years, and each
one is filled with the same almost embarrassing inti-
macy as his comeback book.*

How could he learn all these secrets?

What is his secret?

*Not even the best detective on the planet could have
learned these things.*

*Rumors begin to circulate about St. Romaine. It is
said that he gathers information on vid stars (he will
never again write about a politician; once burned and
all that) and then offers to not write them if the money
is right. The term we want here is* blackmail. *These
are the books he doesn't write. The ones he does write
meanwhile become instant best-sellers. . . .*

St. Romaine is back on top.

*Good old William Bunkley. A neo-fascist to his
glitzy core.*

*And now he's courting beautiful women again,
making all sorts of titillating remarks to the newsies,
and planning more and more new books.*

*Everybody hates him. Everybody lives in terror of
him.*

He loves it. Positively goddamn loves it.

*Which brings us up to last night and to the planet
Tumbleweed, where somebody finally does him in.*

Finally.

The lights came up.

"Pretty swell guy, don't you think?" Brackett said,
smiling, as he looked out over the faces in the room.

Half a dozen other space cops had come in after Daily.

"Yeah," said one of the cops, laughing. "I can't think of more than, say, six or seven million people who'd have wanted to murder him."

"Hell, while I was watching that, *I* wanted to murder him," said an attractive older cop who was finishing the last of her coffee.

"There is a lot of work to do," Brackett said. "We need to reconstruct St. Romaine's entire time on Tumbleweed. We need to know where he went and who came to see him. We need to know if he sent any dispatches off, or if he received any. Daily, Obo, and I will be working on the three likeliest suspects thus far. The rest of you should coordinate all your activities with the central computer so I can follow everything you're doing." He thought of Wade Foster, still in a psychotic state because of the drug, still assumed to be the real killer by millions and millions of kids throughout the Federation. Brackett had to catch the real killer; had to because otherwise, even if the star cops freed Wade Foster, the cry of "cover-up" would be heard throughout the Federation.

A green-tinted cop from the jungles of Rithian I raised his hands. "Lieutenant Brackett, do we have your permission to go to the street dance tonight?"

Brackett smiled. "Only if it's in the line of duty." He looked at Obo. The big guy managed to look both menacing and teddy-bear friendly in his white Western duds. "In fact, I'll bet you find Obo there tonight."

Obo laughed. "Strictly in the line of duty."

Brackett saluted the other cops and said, "We've got a hell of a lot of work ahead of us so just remember, even if you do end up at the street dance tonight, go easy on the alcohol."

The other cops returned his salute.

Brackett, Daily, and Obo were the last to leave the room, bringing the lights down behind them.

"Where do we start?" Daily said.

"I start with the young woman who came in while we were there, you start with St. Romaine's male secretary, and Obo keeps looking into the past of this swami guy."

"Master Mentalist is the proper term."

"Oh, yes, Obo, excuse me. Master Mentalist. How gauche of me."

Obo grinned. Taus loved sarcasm. It was candy for their ears. As he listened, he hummed. A fightin' buckaroo I am, I am.

Brackett nodded as he turned left down the corridor. "Good luck, folks. See you at dinner tonight."

Brackett went to find out what he could about Marcia Tenhold, and why she'd suddenly climbed through St. Romaine's bedroom window back at the cabin.

Chapter Ten

The killer got the idea walking along the edge of the blue, blue waters of the swimming pool.

The killer had always had a droll sense of humor, and this idea proved it.

While Dirk St. Romaine's body parts were safe enough for now, sitting in the cold white interior of his cabin's refrigeration unit, they still made him nervous.

Little by little, the body parts had to be dispersed.

A face appeared in the refrigerator door. The killer's face. Eyes peering inside.

There was a clear plastic bag at the back. It was streaked badly with blood and entrails. This kind of thing could just never be neat so there was no point in being anxious. Murder was usually a bloody business.

My God, the killer had done the best job possible. What more could you ask?

The killer reached in and pulled the bag out.

Despite the refrigeration, the ears, eyes, and hands of the late Dirk St. Romaine had begun to smell. There was the faint taint of blood; the even fainter taint of putrefaction.

But again, the killer had done the best job possible. Sighing, the killer decided to make a game of it.

Isn't that what life is anyway, when you come right down to it, just a silly fucking game? We didn't ask to be players, we don't even know whose idea it was for us to be players, and then the game is abruptly called on account of darkness. Eternal darkness.

D-e-a-t-h, for shit's sake.

The killer reached inside the bag.

The stuff was definitely icky, especially the hand with all the stuff sticking out.

As if he were reaching into a grab bag, the killer decided to choose whatever his fingers next came in contact with.

An ear.

Right by the lobe.

The killer took the ear from the bag—it was stiff and bloody and the refrigeration had given it a kind of slimy coldness—and then zipped up the bag again and put it back in the refrigeration unit.

When the bag was safe inside again, when the door was closed, the killer stood there holding the bloody ear.

The killer thought of all the likely places to take it.

There were so many possibilities.

And then the perfect place came to mind: the French place where all the waiters pretended to speak French. My God, what poseurs.

Yes, that would be the perfect place.

The killer went over to the grinder—he had not, after all, come unprepared—and began feeding the ear into the small opening on top.

How the little motor roared.

How the little mouth of the grinder spat out the pieces of ear in small bits and chunks.

When the killer was done with them, he took another small plastic bag and whisked all the ear parts inside.

It lent a touch of merriment to the otherwise gruesome murder, didn't it—taking all this to the French restaurant?

● ● ●

An hour later, the killer stood in the rear of the restaurant.

Skulking. That was the only word for the way the killer was behaving now, and it was fun.

Skulking. The way villains did on kid-vid shows.

Oh, yes, a regular goddamned villain, and it was exhilarating.

The killer opened the back door and went inside.

The kitchen smelled of heat, grease, hot dishwater, burning butter, and braising meat. The kitchen sounded of cursing, pots and pans clanging, plates breaking on the tiled floor, cursing, and distant shouts as chefs told assistant chefs what they needed. And cursing. And not in French, either, but in the most guttural grunts and groans of English.

There were probably twenty people in the madhouse of a kitchen, most of them affecting the black-and-white checkered pants, white medical jackets, and tall white puffy chef hats of their calling.

Their backs were to the killer.

They were rushing, rushing.

The killer had to hurry. Had to do the job before even one of them turned around, and then get the hell out of here. Unseen.

The killer rushed to one of the stoves where a tall silver pan bubbled like a witches' caldron, some kind of tomato soup, the surface as turbulent as Venus.

Perfect, perfect, perfect.

The killer quickly took the small clear plastic bag, unzipped the top of it, and then scattered the ear parts into the orange bubbling brew.

Except the ear parts didn't sink the way the killer thought they would. They just bobbed there, floating on the surface.

Son of a bitch, you plan and you work hard and you live clean and stuff like this still happened.

It just wasn't fair.

The goddamn ear parts were supposed to goddamn sink.

"Help you with something?"

The killer whirled around, facing a paunchy man in a chef's outfit. "Help you?" the man repeated.

"Just looking around the kitchen. I ate here last night and it was so good, I thought I'd just sort of check it out and—"

"Nobody's allowed back here."

For the first time, the killer noticed that the chef looked pretty mean. Steely blue eyes and some kind of scar on his lantern jaw and big hands that could easily become big fists.

"Well, sorry, I just thought—"

And then the killer glanced once more at the tomato soup.

Floating. Those ear parts were still floating right on the top.

"We're busy now. You'll have to go."

The killer couldn't afford to protest anymore. Or hang around. The chef here was bound to get suspicious.

"Well, you serve wonderful meals."

"Thank you."

"I'll probably eat here again tonight."

"Great."

All the time they were having this little confab, the chef was pushing him toward the back door.

The killer took one last, lone glance back at the bubbling brew of tomato soup.

The whole thing was now entirely in the hands of the gods.

Such a nice little plan: some lard-ass rich guy would be sitting here tonight spooning his soup when he'd notice something kind of chunky in the soup and then he'd call the maître d', who would be most embarrassed and apologetic and then the restaurant *owner would have the bits and pieces floating in the soup analyzed and then they'd find . . .*

Somebody had put somebody's goddamned ear in the tomato soup.

Boy, would they all talk French then. Dirty French.

"See you tonight," the killer said, as the chef opened the back door like a servant.

The chef nodded a relieved good-bye.

The door slammed shut.

The tomato soup bubbled.

The ear parts floated.

All that could be done now was to hope for the best.

The killer hurried away.

Chapter Eleven

For a man who'd spilled more than his share of blood—both human and alien—Brackett had an almost immobilizing fear of hospitals. Instead of going straight to see Marcia Tenhold, he decided to stop and see how Carver was doing, a twelve-minute trip from the "theme" area to the gambling area "downtown."

Ten feet across the threshold, pains started crackling like summer lightning across his chest, he felt his extremities start to go numb, and wasn't his vision starting to fade . . . fade?

But now, Brackett didn't have any choice.

The star cops had moved Carver from St. Romaine's cabin, where Carver had been seized by some kind of sudden and terrible illness that seemed to have something to do with the sparkly dust on his shoulder. . . .

A fat guy dressed as a cowboy clown was handing out balloons in the hospital lobby.

Such people always embarrassed Brackett. Didn't they have any self-respect?

He arced wide in the lobby so the clown wouldn't see him . . . and headed for the elevators.

His luck didn't hold, however.

As he stood there waiting for the elevator doors to open, Brackett saw a white-gloved hand thrust a yellow balloon in his face.

"Have a nice day, sir!" the clown shouted.

Half the lobby turned to look at Brackett, an other-

wise rough, tough guy in the tight Western duds of
an old-time bad-ass . . . holding this big yellow balloon in his hand . . . and talking to this silly-ass
clown.

When the elevator doors opened, Brackett nearly
dived through them.

Unfortunately, the elevator was filled with passen-
gers. Their glances said that they, too, were curious
about why a man like Brackett would be holding a
yellow balloon.

"How is he?" Brackett said.

"Not good," the doctor said.

"Any diagnosis yet?"

"Nothing that's not pure speculation."

They stood in the quiet, polished hallway outside
Carver's room. A pretty nurse squeaked by in her
white oxfords. She smiled at Brackett and he smiled
back. He hadn't been with a woman in months and it
was starting to bother him, not so much sexually as
emotionally. He just liked women.

"Tell me your speculation," Brackett said.

The doctor was a Krausen, one of the so-called
monkey-men who seemed to have a preternatural
disposition to medicine. With his hairy face and
sunken brown eyes and little nose, the doctor did
look a lot like a monkey. No offense.

"Some kind of microbe but apparently it's something that doesn't work on everybody."

"Oh?"

"Obviously, you were all exposed to the same room
as Carver. Yet he was the only one who came down
with seizures."

"Any chemical analysis of the dust yet?"

The doctor shook his simian head. "Afraid not.
We're trying, of course, but the computers just aren't
coming up with anything."

"I'll check in with you around suppertime."

"Fine."

The men walked up to Carver's door and peeked in. The man lay inside some kind of plastic covering. Oxygen was being pumped into his system through two small hoses.

"What's with the coloring?"

"His face?" the doctor asked.

Brackett nodded. Carver looked as if somebody had thrown red paint all over his face.

"We have no idea," the doctor said.

Brackett withdrew from the room and said, "I guess I should ask. What are his survival chances?"

"Not as bad as they were an hour ago but—" He shrugged.

"But what?"

"But still not good."

"Because you don't know what you're dealing with?"

"Exactly."

Brackett shook his head and started over to the elevator.

"I'll talk to you around suppertime," the doctor said, and walked away, his tail switching right to left in the tail hole of his medical smock.

"God, I envy you, Lieutenant."

But John Paul Johansen didn't hear. And hadn't heard anything for many hours now.

The shift had changed. Techs came and went, many of them stopping to say hello to Lieutenant Johansen as they passed the small, self-contained station where Johansen, the boss, did his work.

Now, hearing something on the periphery of his hearing, Johansen looked up from his screen and said, "Pardon me?"

Ria, pretty redheaded Ria, stood next to him. "I said I envy you, sir. Your powers of concentration.

This is the first time you've looked up from your screen since my shift started five hours ago."

"Oh, uh, yes. Thank you." Johansen knew it wasn't the proper response. But he didn't care. He just wanted to get back to his work.

Ria knew better than to push things past this point. She smiled nervously and walked over to her own station, the lab consisting of twelve stations and a large work area in the center used by all. Johansen was famous for his temper. She'd never seen it in action, and didn't plan to.

As for Johansen, he went right back to his screen, muttering to himself as he worked.

A mysterious sparkling dust. Origin unknown.

But not for long; not for long.

Feverishly, Johansen punched keys, watching the screen shift constantly.

Soon he'd know the source of the mysterious sparkling dust; soon.

And not many months after, he'd be on vids throughout the Federation, humbly accepting his Moskowitz.

Humbly.

Chapter Twelve

Daily had never planned on being a virgin at twenty-eight years of age. It had just happened —or *not* happened that way. Twice in college, she'd almost done the deed but then both young men proved to be such jerks (ten years ago there'd been a movement to put women back in the home, and both young men favored it) that she declined. Then there'd been that dashing young Star Navy ensign from Arcturus but the night before they were to spend the weekend together, she learned that he was married. She would not give herself to a married man. . . .

Then Dreesen had come along and so she'd slept with him and it had been fine and good—if not quite wonderful—but then he went and ruined it by trying to push her into marriage.

She thought of all these things as she hurried through the west end of Tumbleweed City. Now that it was late afternoon, the casinos were just turning on their laser lights. Giant laser cowboys twirled giant laser ropes; giant laser cowgirls tossed out giant laser betting chips. And giant laser six-shooters fired giant laser coins into the air.

It was melancholy time, even here in the city, long afternoon shadows making all the lights brighter, tourists starting to show the first signs of fatigue, wanting to get back to their hotel rooms to lie down or wash up, to re-create a sense of home within the boundaries of all this relentless fun.

She didn't want to marry Dreesen. She was not in love with Dreesen. She—

She had to clear her mind.

She had an interview to conduct.

A very serious interview, one that might have great bearing on the murder of Dirk St. Romaine.

And damn Dreesen, anyway—.

Matthew Pendrake, Dirk St. Romaine's personal secretary, whom she was going to see at the moment, had moved from a cabin near his former employer to one of the downtown hotels.

Now, as she rode up to his room in a quick glistening 'chute, she scanned the backgrounder she'd been given.

Pendrake was an off-worlder, from one of the minor systems out near Vanik 1V. He was thirty-six years old, had spent much of his working life as a newsie writer, and had covered three wars, including the bloody and seemingly endless (and so-called) End of Eternity War, in which more than 6 million civilians had died. She couldn't match these facts to her impression of the slight, rather prim man she'd met back in St. Romaine's cabin.

But then—and she'd be the first to admit it—Daily was an unmitigated sexist.

While she didn't like men who were loud, boorish, or bullyish, she did like men who were, well, *men*.

She walked down a narrow corridor smelling sweetly of cleaning solvent and knocked on Pendrake's door.

She'd phoned ahead for this interview so he answered immediately.

She got a very different impression of the man this time.

True, he remained short, blond, blue-eyed to the point of innocence but now there was something subtly different about him.

"Hi."

"Hi," Daily said.

"I can offer you coffee or vodka."

"Coffee," she said.

He smiled and for the first time she noticed that he wasn't bad looking at all. "I was hoping you'd say vodka."

He stepped aside, ushered her in, and closed the door behind her.

The room had a view of the river, with sailboats drifting lazily across water, which had taken on a copper hue in the setting sun.

After he'd left the room to get her coffee from the kitchen area, she got up and drifted over to the window, brushing against a partly open closet door as she did so. With instinctive curiosity, she glanced inside at a full rack of clothes. The outfit that struck her attention was a dark three-piece suit. From the same hanger dangled a black male wig and what appeared to be a full black mustache. But then she shrugged and thought of how fashionable it was becoming to go out at night disguised as somebody else. This was probably why Pendrake kept such an outfit in his closet.

And then, abruptly and with no warning, she had a headache. A terrible one.

She went over and sat down again. Pendrake returned with her coffee and seated himself.

Just sitting here, staring at Pendrake, a dull throbbing began behind her eyes and at the pressure points of her temples.

"How's the coffee?" he asked.

"Fine."

"More sugar?"

"Fine, really," Daily said. Then she realized that somehow he'd gotten in charge of the situation here.

She should be asking the questions, not him.

"I wanted to talk to you about Dirk St. Romaine."

"I assumed as much."

"Have you thought of anybody else who might have wanted him dead?"

Matthew Pendrake smiled. "Millions and millions of suspects. Literally. He reveled in being hated. It fulfilled some pathetic need in him. He hated himself and somehow it made it easier for others to hate him, too."

"You were in the End of Eternity War?"

"Oh, so you are a cop, after all."

"Pardon me?"

"You're so pretty, so fresh. And dressed up in that Western outfit . . . well, I forget sometimes that you really are a cop."

"I see."

"So you've done a backgrounder on me?"

"Yes."

"I take it then I'm a suspect?"

"I wouldn't put it that way, exactly."

He smiled again. "Then how would you put it?"

Now she smiled. "An innocent bystander until proven otherwise."

Suddenly, the headache bloomed in her head like a neutron explosion.

She started to pitch forward, darkness rushing at her.

Somehow Pendrake was there, helping her over to the couch, helping her lie down.

My God, what was going on here?

"I'll get you a glass of water. You just lie still," Pendrake said.

There was just a hint of panic in his voice, as why should there not be?

A perfectly healthy twenty-eight-year-old woman is sitting there asking questions and suddenly she faints?

What was happening here, anyway?

Despite her pain and chaos, Daily felt deeply embarrassed as Pendrake rushed to get her water.

• • •

"Miss Tenhold?"

The first thing she did when she saw him was frown. Given all the things he'd learned about her, he could see why.

"May I help you Lieutenant Brackett?"

"I'd like to talk to you."

"I'm afraid that's impossible. I'm just on my way out for dinner."

Apparently this was true.

She looked wonderful in a buff blue cocktail dress that lent a certain color to her slender but soft shoulders and her dark, luxurious short hair.

"Couldn't we do this tomorrow?"

"I'm afraid not."

She sighed. "I really do have a date."

"I'm sure you do. But you've also got a legal problem."

"Oh? What's that?"

"Everything you told me is a lie. You don't work for Larry Bowman, the boxer. You don't have a brother. And your name isn't Marcia Tenhold."

She surprised him by starting to cry softly. He had the sense the tears were for his sake.

He took her elbow, gently, and pointed her in the direction of the veranda. "It's a nice view. Why don't we go out there?"

She nodded.

Five minutes later, she said, "He destroyed my father, St. Romaine did. In three lines. Three lines in a book about an actor my father didn't even know. St. Romaine implied that the actor was connected to the crime lords, and that one of his contacts was a man much like my father, a leading industrialist. He didn't use my father's name. He didn't have to. The press used my father's name for him."

She was long through crying. Pure, clean anger

had replaced sorrow. "My father took his private jet up and crashed it into the mountain. I inherited millions of credits but they've never been enough to replace my father."

"Are you telling me that you killed St. Romaine?"

She smiled at him. She was one of those delicate creatures who seem to be as much fawn as human. "No, and that's the irony. I'd been planning to kill him for months. I could have hired his death but I didn't want anybody else to have the pleasure. Anyway, when I got to his cabin last night, he was already dead. It taught me something, though."

"What's that?"

"As much as I hated him, I don't think anybody deserves to die the way he did."

"It was gruesome, that's for sure."

"Even for you?"

He laughed. "Just because I'm a cop doesn't mean I traded in my humanity. Or had my stomach lined with lead. That was a very vicious murder."

She sighed and looked out at the rolling bluffs and hills to the north. A quarter moon shone through the aqua-colored dusk. The temperature had fallen seven degrees in the past hour.

She hugged her arms tight across her chest. "You know when I lied and said I had a brother?"

"Yes."

She glanced up at him with her silky brown gaze. "I wish I did have a brother. I feel lonely. Do you ever feel lonely, Lieutenant Brackett?"

"All the time."

"You don't have a wife, then?"

His face tensed. "I did once."

"What happened to her?"

He pointed to a large plane just now silhouetted against the round orange sinking sun. "That's really something to see, isn't it?"

"You're not going to tell me about your wife?"

"No, I'm not, Miss Tenhold."

"You sound angry."

"I'd just like to change the subject. Anyway, I'm the one who's supposed to be asking the questions."

"I didn't kill him."

"I'll send somebody to search your room."

"For what?"

"For evidence that you're lying."

"They'll be looking for what? Blood? Things like that?"

He nodded. "Yes, things like that."

She touched him on the forearm. It felt better than he wanted it to. "I'm sorry if I hurt you in some way. Asking you about your wife, I mean."

He nodded. "Thank you."

"Do you have dinner plans?"

"You have a date, Miss Tenhold, in case you forgot."

"I'm sure he didn't wait. He's rich and handsome and when you're rich and handsome, you're also impatient. I'm sure he's with somebody else by now."

"Well, I guess I wouldn't know about being rich and handsome."

She laughed. "You just want a compliment."

He smiled, too. "Maybe you're right."

She slid her arm through his. "Can you officially escort a suspect to dinner?"

"I guess we're about to find out, aren't we?"

And with that, they walked off the veranda and found the elevator.

Chapter Thirteen

Daily opened her eyes. She had no idea where she was. Her head pounded.

"Hi. Remember me?"

A face peered into her vision.

"Matthew Pendrake."

"Oh. Right."

"You're in my hotel room."

"Right." Vaguely it was starting to come back to her.

"You were asking me some questions and then you fainted."

She closed her eyes a moment. Pendrake. Hotel room. Questions.

Then she remembered the murder of Dirk St. Romaine.

She struggled to sit up.

Matthew Pendrake helped her.

By the time she was upright and leaning against the arm of the couch, Pendrake held a cool drink out to her.

"This should help."

"Thank you."

He went back to his chair and sat down. "You scared me for a minute. I was afraid something serious had happened."

"I don't know what happened. I just . . . blacked out."

"You're probably tired. That's how I always get on these vacation worlds. Try to pack too much in."

She sipped her iced tea and then stood up.

Her knees were wobbly.

"Are you all right?"

"Yes."

She was starting to feel embarrassed now. She had completely surrendered any authority she might have had with this man. God, passing out in front of him. "I'll be back tomorrow, Mr. Pendrake."

He smiled at her, obviously appreciative of her good looks. "I'd like that."

She chose to pretend he wasn't flirting with her. First she passes out and then the guy she's supposed to be questioning—a guy who's clearly a suspect— starts coming on to her.

Wonderful.

She set the iced-tea glass down and started to the door.

Another wave of darkness rolled up over her eyes, threatening to capsize her again.

But she made fists of her hands and pistons of her legs.

She force-marched herself to the door, put a hand on the knob, and stepped out into the hallway.

"Are you all right?"

"I'm fine, Mr. Pendrake." There'd been a little touch of irritation in her voice. She felt he was starting to exploit her situation. Female officer doesn't feel well and so he starts playing the classic macho male, which, considering his diminutive size, was sort of pathetic.

"Good luck," Pendrake said, and closed the door.

She walked to the elevator.

A couple of times, her knees started to buckle, and she felt the odd rushing dizziness lap at her consciousness again, but she was no pantywaist, not Daily. She started her forced march again and made it to the elevator with no real problems at all.

And then started feeling cooler, calmer, and steadier.

She felt good enough suddenly to walk back into Pendrake's, grab him by the lapels, throw him up against the wall the way Mike Hammer did on those old vids, and slap a few answers out of him.

Of course, if she did that she'd get an official reprimand from Carnes.

And would be suspended without pay for two months.

And would be filling out official forms for the next six months.

And would have a "See Command Central" designation on her computer record, Command Central being the sure sign that somewhere in the past, this particular officer had not only screwed up but screwed up badly.

No, tempting as it was, she wouldn't go back to Pendrake's and throw him around his hotel room.

But she was curious about why she felt so much better so suddenly.

But then she quit worrying about it and just took it for granted that whatever fleeting malady had afflicted her, it was gone.

She stepped onto the elevator, gave the robo the proper voice instruction, and fell eighty-six floors.

Bagdar was a thief. He was also, though not necessarily in this order, a loner, a loser, a pervert, and a patriot. His home planet was Craknik, a minor world famous mostly for a species of suicidal birds that kept flying straight into the sun until the scorching heat killed them. The birds had inspired any number of troubadors to write rather idealized songs about them. In fact, the birds psychotically attacked any species not its own, and had been known to drag off and eat Terran children. But still, the troubadors liked to sing their wan little campfire songs about them.

But Bagdar the thief had an entirely different notion of his home planet.

First of all, the Craknikians, a squat humanoid race, loved to fight. And second of all, they loved to write and sing endless drear songs that were all about, naturally enough, their battles. It was said that one Craknikian ballad lasts more than three days. This may be a falsehood but when listening to a Craknikian song, one got the idea that three days had just passed.

So whenever Bagdar thought of Craknik, he thought, logically enough, of Craknikian songs, and whenever he thought of Craknikian songs, he got all teary eyed.

The dear old mother planet etc.

He was thinking about a particularly bloody and sad war ballad when he ran into the only other Craknikian on Tumbleweed (at least as far as he knew), a man named Raskar, who was also a thief.

Raskar was just weaving his way out of a drak-knee bar, drakknee being the cheapest (and foulest) way for lowlifes to obliterate their senses.

Bagdar was surprised Raskar even recognized him, reeling in the dying sunlight, reeking of drak-knee.

Both men leaned toward each other. Bagdar jammed one of his fingers up Raskar's nose, and Raskar did likewise with Bagdar, and so, with the formal greeting out of the way, Raskar said, "You look troubled, my friend."

"I am troubled," Bagdar said, shaking his burnoose, drawing his dusty robes tighter about him now that the day's warmth was fading. "I'm about to do something entirely against my nature."

"Gods!" Raskar said, and then reeled off a list of

possible perversities that Bagdar might be thinking of performing.

But Bagdar only shook his burnoose again. "Nothing so exotic, I'm afraid." He frowned. "I'm going to help the star cops solve a crime."

"What!"

"Yes. Truly these are the facts. The writer Dirk St. Romaine who was found slain in his cabin?"

"Yes."

"I think I saw the person who killed him coming and going from there. At the time"—here he lowered his voice—"at the time, I was in the cabin across the way. The people were out and I was, well, I was filling my sac." At which point, he swept back his robe and proudly showed Raskar the fleshy sac that grew from his side, much like a kangaroo's pouch. "This was brimming full when I happened to look out the window and see."

"But they will arrest you!"

Which was possibly true, Bagdar knew. All cops throughout the Federation were only too eager to arrest Craknikians because most Craknikians, despite their protests to the contrary, were thieves. It was that simple.

What are you doing on Tumbleweed? How long have you been here? How many cabins have you robbed? How many tourists have you pickpocketed? The questions would be endless, and Bagdar could not protest his innocence because he was not innocent.

But—

"But I have no choice."

"No choice?"

"You know our code. No violence. And if I let a killer go free, then I am participating in the act of violence, too. Much as if I killed him myself."

"But you know the nickname for the star cops—

'Pigs in Space'! And well deserved it is, too. They hate all Craknikians just for existing."

Bagdar was already drifting away, toward the hotel where he'd been told the star cops were staying while planetside.

"I wish you luck, my cousin," Raskar said, now shaking his own burnoose. "I still think you've lost your senses."

But now Bagdar wanted to get it over with, see the star cops, describe the person he'd seen inside St. Romaine's cabin, and then go back to a little more stealing before his vacationer's visa ended tomorrow night.

Bagdar now looked at Raskar, bowed formally from the waist, wriggled his little finger in the air, and then jammed it up his nose.

Raskar, also performing the Craknikian good-bye salute, did likewise.

Bagdar then hurried into the deepening shadows, moving inexorably to the hotel where he'd find the cops.

He hoped that none of his ancestors were watching him from above.

He was about to do something even more shameful than any perversion he'd ever performed.

And that was saying something.

Chapter Fourteen

Obo always liked the idea of combining business and pleasure. It seemed the natural order of things. He didn't even have to feel guilty about it since the force generally encouraged such practices while on a vacation planet. What better cover was there than whooping it up with the natives?

For this reason, Obo whistled as he walked down the crowded, twilight street on his way to the hotel where Ahmed, the Master Mentalist, would be appearing tonight. And what was he whistling? "I'm A Fightin' Buckaroo, I Am, I Am."

Only one thing had spoiled his mood this evening: he'd happened to catch thirty seconds of a vid editorial in which a network spokesperson was berating the star cops for having an alleged murderer like Wade Foster recruit young men and women to the force.

The spokesperson had quoted at length from Foster's confession.

The egg-sucking tinhorn, Obo thought as the image of the TV pretty boy came to his mind again.

She was waiting in the lobby. She wore a white blouse and Western skirt and cute little Western boots. Lyra, her name was, and she was a receptionist at the hotel only until she could get her acting career going. And God, did she love star cops. And God, did she feel sorry for Wade Foster. And God, just let anybody try to say anything against the force. She'd take her cute little fist and hit him right in the eye, she would.

Obo got all this even before the waiter came over to take their order. He was happy she knew he was a cop, and was glad he didn't have to be undercover tonight.

Groupie, he thought. That's the word for such a young woman.

He'd heard of them. Some cops liked to brag about (a) having the most groupies, (b) having the prettiest groupies, and (c) having the kinkiest groupies.

Obo, who was a true feminist, believing completely in the equality of the sexes, wondered why macho star cops who were indiscreet enough to discuss their sex lives anyway—why didn't these guys boast about (a) having the most intelligent groupies, (b) having the most sensitive groupies, or (c) having the best-read groupies?

"God, it's so thrilling being here."

"I'm thrilled, too."

"You are, really, Obo? You're not just saying that?"

"Oh, no. You're a nice person and this is a nice nightclub and it's enjoyable being here."

"But you said thrilling."

"Well, enjoyable *and* thrilling," Obo said.

She giggled.

The waiter came and showed them menus.

Obo ordered seafood (he could eat anything that didn't have a sweet face, such as a cow or a lamb or a cute little piggie) and she ordered Tumbleweed's most famous concoction, something called Sonofabitch Stew, which was a blooded meat eater's delight, containing such things as heart, liver, kidneys, and brains of various hoofed animals. Allegedly, this had been considered a real treat by the cowboys of earth in the 1800s.

Obo looked around. This was called The Campfire Room, and it was all got up like a campfire of old, with the table spread in a semicircle around a massive fireplace, an eight-piece band complete with slide guitar in the shadows to the west, and a full contingent of waiters and waitresses duded up in cowboy clothes, as were most of the diners. Obo had showered and changed into a different Western outfit, a brown costume that blended nicely with his green skin. This one didn't have as much fringe as the one he'd worn to shoot the android-villain earlier this morning.

"Are you still interested in Ahmed?" Lyra said.

"Yes. Why?"

"Well, something strange happened this afternoon."

"What was that?"

"Somebody saw him out on the ledge of his hotel room today."

"What floor is he on?"

"The ninety-sixth."

Obo was afraid of heights. He couldn't imagine what it would be like to stand on the ledge of the ninety-sixth floor. "Was he going to jump?"

"No. It looked like somebody had come in his room and he had no choice except to hide on the ledge."

"You saw this?"

"No, but one of the bellboys did and he told me about it. He was using binoculars. Management assigned him to scanning the exterior of the buildings. We still get people who use those fake wings once in a while, and our insurance just won't cover those lawsuits." A few years earlier, somebody had invented a pair of wings called Pegasuses, which enabled adventurous types to jump off tall buildings and float around like little birds. That is, if the updraft was strong enough. If not . . . well, their survivors got very angry, hired themselves some ambulance-chasin' egg-suckin' lawyer, and sued the collective ass off those unfortunate enough to own the building.

"So Ahmed eventually went back in?"

"Eventually."

"Did the bellboy get a chance to see who was in the room?"

"He said it was a short man with very black hair and a black mustache and a black suit."

"He left without seeing Ahmed?"

"Apparently."

"And what did Ahmed do?"

"Just came back in from the ledge."

"He didn't complain to the management?"

"No."

Obo thought a moment. "He didn't complain to the force, either."

"Everything must be fine now."

"Why's that?"

"Because one of the staff saw him in here earlier getting everything ready for his act tonight."

"I see." Obo nodded to the stage. "What time is he scheduled to perform?"

"Another hour or so."

Obo pointed to his drink. "I'd better go easy, then."

"I thought Taus liked alcohol."

"We like it too well. That's the problem."

She sipped her own drink—something called a cactus cocktail, well suited to the motif of the room—and then said, "Could you do me a favor, Obo?"

"I hope so. What did you have in mind?"

"Do you have a badge?"

"You mean a police badge?"

"Yes."

"Sure." He pulled out his wallet. Nestled inside the fold was a four-pointed star. Made of pure silver, it shone in the flickering firelight.

"It's beautiful."

"It is rather nice, isn't it?"

"Would you wear it?"

"Wear it?"

"Yes. You know . . . on your chest."

"On my chest?"

"Yes, so people would know you're a star cop."

"You're not joking?"

"Oh, no. Not at all. What's the point of going out with a star cop if nobody *knows* he's a star cop."

"I see." He wanted to say: Gee, I thought it was the fact that I'm a nice, big, amiable guy. He wanted to say: Gee, I thought it was that you felt some kind of romantic spark—the same kind of romantic spark I feel. He wanted to say: Don't you know it's awfully sexist to use people this way?

Instead, he said, "Like this?" And with that, he pinned the silver star to his chest.

She clapped her hands together like a small, delighted child. "It's wonderful!" she cried. "It's wonderful!"

Obo had never felt so alone in all his life.

Xenon was the name of the world from which the mysterious sparkling dust came. The first humans ever to come in contact with the dust—which was blown down from sand-covered mountains on the eastern plains of the planet— were brought to Xenon in two Federation ships, and a few members of both survey parties had had identical reactions to the dust: high fevers, paralysis, dementia, and (in at least two individual cases) death. Certain immune systems were simply not able to fight off the deleterious effects of the dust—and one of those failed systems obviously belonged to Carver, the star cop who had been stricken in Dirk St. Romaine's room.

Obviously, the dust from the planet Xenon caused an allergic reaction in some Federation races.

John Paul Johansen took all this in at his work

station. He permitted himself his first smile in precisely seven hours and thirty-five minutes.

But the smile was short-lived because his work was far from over.

Now he needed to find out how such dust could possibly have been transported from Xenon to Tumbleweed.

As the shift changed for the third time since John Paul Johansen had seated himself in the lab, he read more about Xenon.

Nearly a century ago, a wealthy man had erected a vast scientific center on the western edge of Xenon. It was his notion to perfect telepathic powers in human beings. He took orphans who tested high in ESP powers and brought them here and fed them and educated them and pampered them—and then brought them along as ESPers. This went on for eight generations. Unfortunately, the majority of the students went insane and committed suicide. A group of them eventually formed a mind link and caused the scientific center itself to explode. Those students who survived scattered themselves throughout the Federation. The computer concluded with: IT IS RUMORED THAT MORE THAN THREE DOZEN TELEPATHS SURVIVED AND ARE WALKING AROUND ON FEDERATED WORLDS TODAY. IT IS ALSO RUMORED THAT THE CURIOUS SPARKLING DUST BLOWN DOWN FROM THE MOUNTAINS ENHANCES THEIR ESP ABILITIES, AND THAT THESE SURVIVING TELEPATHS THEREFORE RETURN FREQUENTLY (AND SECRETLY) TO XENON DISGUISED AS TOURISTS INTERESTED ONLY IN THE GREAT HUNTS FOR WHICH THE WORLD HAS BECOME FAMOUS.

As he read this, John Paul Johansen became so excited, he began to tremble.

There was a very good chance that the killer was not only a murderer but one of the legendary telepaths of Xenon as well.

Right here on Tumbleweed, walking undetected

among all other creatures, was a true and genuine telepath!

"Are you all right, sir?"

"Huh?" Johansen swung his head up and saw a young recruit standing there.

"I asked if you were all right. You were making . . . funny noises, sir."

Johansen waved the recruit away. "My noises are my own business!"

"Yes, sir," the recruit said, looking back at the small knot of lab workers who had also heard the strange, excited mewling noises that had been coming from deep in Johansen's throat.

Maybe the time had finally arrived when Lieutenant John Paul Johansen was finally going to have that complete and total mental breakdown everybody had been expecting for years.

But Johansen paid them no heed.

He was already back working at his screen.

With any luck, he was soon to discover not only the killer but a real live telepath as well!

Chapter Fifteen

Corporal Kettering was watching a cop show when Bagdar came in.

Star cops liked to make fun of such shows, and probably with good reason. On the vids, everything looked easy, even dying.

Take a guy who'd just been shot—cop or criminal, it didn't matter—what did he do? ... He lay in the street bleeding to death, saying something clever, polished, and beautifully delivered.

Now, that was pretty unlikely, because when a guy got creamed that way, his system would start to do all sorts of unpleasant things, including fouling itself, and he'd start to come undone.

No speeches.

No pithy lines.

No perfectly formed words, complete with dramatic gestures.

The victim lay there, one more pitiful goddamn animal, and died.

Corporal Kettering didn't care about all this, however. He saw cop shows as a pretty wonderful way to pass the time because, despite a lot of evidence to the contrary, that was just how he saw himself.

As a hero.

Just the way star cops were on the vid.

He believed this because he wasn't quite twenty-four years old, because he'd never seen anybody die, and because his life had never been threatened.

Jennifer Daily had been one kind of virgin; James K. Kettering a virgin of a very different sort.

A knock sounded. Kettering looked up. He was guarding the equipment various members of the force had left behind after an afternoon of interrogation. And he had all the things he needed for such sentry duty—snack food, a comfortable chair, and a sixty-one-inch vid.

As he went to the door, Kettering's right hand dropped to his blaster. Nobody on the force had used a blaster for nearly six decades, but Kettering liked them because they fit snugly into a holster and consequently he could wear them slung low, the way the old gunnies used to. Plus, the blaster and holster went well with the rest of Kettering's getup: the white hat, the red kerchief, the blue shirt with the imitation pearl buttons, the dungarees, and the heavy leather chaps. The latter were an especially nice touch, Kettering thought, especially the way they brushed across the arch of his genuine alligator cowboy boots.

By the time he reached the door, Kettering was not only riding his hand on his blaster, he had also affected a discernibly bowlegged gait, one redolent of years spent bustin' broncs and dodging tumblin' tumbleweed.

Kettering took his blaster out and then ripped the door backward.

A small, swarthy man in a white tuxedo stood there. "I'm Alphonse."

"Who?"

"Alphonse. The maître d'."

"Yes?"

"You are a star cop?"

"Yup."

"There is a Craknikian man here who would like to speak with you."

"About what?"

It was clear by now that the man was trembling. Kettering had forgotten to take his blaster out of the man's face.

"Oh," Kettering said, "sorry."

Captain Carnes had many times warned Kettering about frightening well-behaved citizens. One or two more reprimands and the captain would never let Kettering venture off the precinct ship.

"Send him in," Kettering said.

The man in the white tuxedo bowed and said, "As you wish."

"I am Bagdar."

"How can I help you?"

"The murder. Dirk St. Romaine?"

"Yes."

"I may have seen the killer."

"My God. Come in, sir."

Kettering stood aside for the stout man in the burnoose and flowing robes. Craknikians kept to their native garb except when they were working the crowds. Then they always wore whatever attire made them least conspicuous.

Kettering led the man over to the interrogation table, pointed to a seat, and said, "I need to vid this."

"Very well."

"You really think you may have seen the killer?" Kettering sounded as gosh-wow as any other twelve-year-old.

"I really think so, yes, sir."

Kettering arranged the vid equipment, did a quick check to make certain everything was functioning, identified for the machine who was being interrogated and on what date and in connection with what case, and then Kettering sat down across the table from Bagdar and immediately had an image of himself getting a precinct award from Captain Carnes. *Carnes pinning the medal on him. The entire precinct bursting into spontaneous applause and then getting to its feet. And then the force theme song being played over the auditorium speakers and grown, even grizzled men unable to help themselves, breaking into tears as Kettering, up there on the stage, saluted the Federation flag. My God.*

"Sir?"

"Yes."

"Are you all right?"

"Pardon?"

"I asked if you were all right," Bagdar said.

"Oh. Yes." Kettering felt himself blush. Sometimes he got so carried away with his thoughts . . . "Tell me about this man you saw in St. Romaine's cabin."

And so Bagdar told him.

Of course, in this version, Bagdar hadn't been across the street looting a cabin, he'd merely been strolling by, a beautiful night and all that.

And just happened to be glancing in the window when . . .

"When I saw him."

"Describe him carefully, Bagdar. This is very important."

Bagdar thought a moment. "He was about my height, I guess, and slender, and he had very black hair and a very black mustache and he wore a very white shirt with a very black tie, and a very black three-piece suit."

"And he was doing what, exactly, when you saw him?"

"Just coming out the door."

"Did he look nervous?"

"Very."

"Did you see a weapon in his hand?"

"No."

"Did you see blood anywhere on his person?"

"No."

"Did he see you?"

"No."

"You kept walking?"

Bagdar hesitated. He had to be careful not to give away the fact that he'd actually been in the cabin across the street. "Yes."

"And this was last night?"

"Yes."

"About what time?"

"Eleven, approximately."

"Would you recognize the man if you saw him again?"

"Absolutely."

"Is there anything else you'd like to add?"

Bagdar thought a long moment. He did not wish to appear foolish in front of this cop. Craknikians appeared foolish in general. Bagdar did not wish to add to their already unfortunate reputation. "Perhaps I should mention the motorbike."

"What motorbike?"

"The one the man in black got onto."

"You know this for certain?"

"Yes."

"Why were you hesitant to tell me?"

"I, uh, did not want you to get the wrong idea, sir."

"About what?"

"About me. I am not by nature a nosy person."

"I see."

"I just sensed that something was wrong and so I hid behind a tree and watched this man get onto a motorbike."

"Was there anything special about this bike?"

"It was a convertible. You know, it could be used on the ground with its two wheels, or it could be used as a hovercraft in the sky. There's a name for them."

"Fliers."

"Quite. Fliers."

"Customs doesn't let tourists bring their own

transportation. That means that this man either rented it or borrowed it from somebody."

"Or stole it," Bagdar said, and then, realizing the implications of his words, hastened to add, "not that I would know about such things."

"Of course not." Kettering was taking notes. There were only four or five places in Tumbleweed City that rented such vehicles. He'd start right away searching for the place that had dealt with the man in black. "Is there anything else you would like to add?"

"No, sir, that is all I can think of at the moment."

"I may want to contact you again. Why don't you tell me where you're staying?"

Bagdar was flustered. He had already drawn far too much attention to himself. He had no desire to give the star cop his local address. The last thing he wanted was a follow-up visit.

"I'm afraid I can't tell you, sir."

Kettering looked up from his notes. "You can't tell me where you're staying?"

"No, sir, I'm afraid not."

"Why?"

"Because . . . my friend is a lady."

"So?"

"A married lady. Her husband is out of town."

"Oh."

"And if she should find out that I told anyone . . ."

Kettering took a card from his clipboard and handed it to Bagdar. "Then you call me. Around midnight tonight. I may have some more questions."

"Yes, sir, I will be only too happy to call you."

Bagdar stood up, swept his dusty robes around him, righted his tilting burnoose, and then gave a small head bow in the direction of the star cop.

"He is a cold-blooded killer, this man. I pray that you capture him soon."

"Thanks for your help. Can you see yourself out?"

"Oh, yes; yes, sir."

Kettering hadn't been this excited since he'd put on his Junior Space Force costume back in ninth grade.

He started hearing the applause again; seeing Captain Carnes, grinning as nobody had ever seen him grin before, pinning on the medal.

Kettering stood up.

He was personally going to check out every flier rental place in Tumbleweed.

What was it they always said on the vid cop shows?

Oh, yes: he was going to take this town apart if he needed to.

Take this whole town apart.

Hell, maybe someday they'd have a vid show based on his life.

"Kettering: Star Cop." And then there'd be this real neat music and then Kettering would be running down a shadowy alley chasing a bad guy and . . .

But right now he had to go check out some flier rentals.

On the way out of the hotel, he wondered if he should think about getting an agent any time soon.

God, imagine: your own agent.

He punched in for a replacement guard, saying he wasn't feeling well. Then he left.

The night was hot and humid and stank of the flesh of a thousand worlds.

Soon enough, Kettering forgot all about show business and went about his work. Yokel that he sometimes was, he was also a damned good cop.

Chapter Sixteen

Halfway through dinner, high on a rocky bluff overlooking a wide blue bend in the river, Marcia Tenhold looked right at Brackett and said, "You haven't been with a woman in a long time, have you?"

He paused midbite—he kept trying to be a veggie (he understood that all life was sacred; he understood it in the abstract, anyway)—and said, "It shows, huh?"

She smiled. "A little bit."

This restaurant had to be one of the few on the entire planet that didn't incorporate some kind of Western motif into its decor. Instead, it was a vast dining room with small tables covered with white starched tablecloths, each table lit by a single candle flickering in the darkness. For once, waiters didn't call women "ma'am" or men "pardner." As entertainment, there was a piano man, whose tastes ran to old Earth tunes by Gershwin and Cole Porter and Frank Loesser.

"What was she like?"

"Who?"

"The woman who broke your heart."

"Oh, she didn't break my heart."

"No?"

"No. She died."

"Oh, God, Brackett, I'm sorry. I shouldn't have stuck my nose in."

"It's all right." He pointed to the wine bottle.

"Please," she said.

When he was finished pouring, he looked out through the long, wide window that overlooked the river below. The stars seemed so close they looked fake. On the other side of the canyon stood a lone coyote, no doubt imported from Earth, who stood on four spindly legs watching them out of his vast, eternal loneliness. Brackett knew how he felt.

"Do you want to hear about her?"

"I'd love to. Because she obviously meant so much to you."

"I wasn't always a star cop, you know."

"Oh? What did you do before becoming a cop?"

"I was a con man. And I killed some people."

She tried hard not to seem surprised. But she didn't make it. Not quite.

"Is that really true?"

"It's really true."

"You just killed people?"

"Not 'people' in the way you mean. I killed others involved in criminal activities, the same way I was."

"But they had bodies and souls, too."

"Bodies, I'll grant you. But I wouldn't bet on them having souls. Not some of the ones I knew, anyway."

"How many do you think you killed?"

He shrugged. "I really didn't keep track. At the time, it didn't seem all that important."

As he spoke, some of the old coldness, the old hardness came back to him, the way he'd been before his wife died and he realized he'd been living on the wrong side of the law.

She watched the brutal planes of his face there in the soft light of the candle.

"You're really a tough guy, aren't you?"

"Not anymore," he said. "I used to be." He shook his head. "Sometimes, I don't even like to think about it."

"You were going to tell me about her."

"Yes . . . yes, I was, wasn't I?" Brackett said.

And so that's just what he did.

Told her all about his wife, including the almost unbelievably grisly way she'd died.

Daily was closing in on Pendrake.

She'd been following him for the past half hour, ever since he'd left his hotel. After leaving his room and taking the elevator down, she'd paused for a strawberry beverage at a fountain, and there suddenly was Pendrake, rushing through the lobby. She was very curious about his destination. She was too good an investigator to let a little fainting spell get in her way. She started following him.

He'd turned out to be just as sleazy as she'd suspected, heading straight for the triple-X section of the city, down where the sidewalks were filthy and the live peep shows even more so.

Dinner for Pendrake turned out to be a maya snake, which he bought from a corner vendor. You crushed the heads of the snakes while they were still wriggling and then you began feeding the snake down your gullet before it had quit twitching.

She stood across the street from him, in the heat, in the neon, in the curses, in the spittle, in the sweat, in the jism of this filthy section of town and watched him tilt his head back and gulp the snake down.

And she wanted to vomit.

God, eating maya snakes made her sick.

She shuddered, and just as she did so some derelict, walking crab-wise, reeking of his own filth, bumped against her and copped a cheap feel of her shapely bottom. She would have turned around and slapped him but she didn't dare draw attention to herself.

She had to content herself with swearing at him under her breath.

You dirty little asshole.

It didn't make her feel a lot better.

Then Pendrake was moving again and so was she.

They walked twenty-five blocks.

She counted every one of them.

Pendrake might be small but he was mighty.

Daily liked to think she was in good condition but by the time Pendrake stopped in front of the theater, she knew better.

She was sweat-covered and her breath was ragged. She wanted to sit down on the curb and guzzle something icy. To hell with the perverts. If they wanted to ogle her, let them ogle.

But Pendrake . . . God, Pendrake looked as if he were out for nothing more than a casual stroll.

He stood beneath the old-fashioned electric marquee staring up at the words that had been set there crookedly:

LIVE TONIGHT:
MYND-GIRL

She stood on the corner—grease, cigarette smoke, heat, urine, and melting asphalt stirring up her allergies—watching him suddenly look over his shoulder.

And stare right at her.

She tried to duck behind a lamppost but it was too late. Damage already done.

But how had he known she was there?

With no warning whatsoever—and apparently for no reason at all—he'd just turned around and . . .

Stared at her.

He went up to the box office, handed over the proper credits, and went inside.

Did she have any choice but to follow?

"Looking for somebody?" the cashier said.

"I . . . uh . . . want a ticket."

"You?"

"Yes. One."

"But you're a—"

"I'm well aware what I am."

"No offense, but—"

Theaters that presented Mynd-Girls were considered the last bastion of male chauvinism. While the species was a humanoid form, albeit an almost ludicrously resplendent one, they allegedly offered more than mere physical thrills. The owner of Mynd-Girls claimed that their stars could tap directly into the minds of the men in the audience, thereby enhancing ecstacy. Mynd-Girls did have low-grade telepathic powers, it seemed, at least enough to put a "buzzing" effect into the minds of the toothless old perverts watching them, but nothing compared to the powers of real telepaths.

"No offense, but I'm a woman."

"Uh, yes."

"I'm also," Daily said, "a vid reporter."

The girl had a sad, seedy face. Now she looked scared. If the theater got raided, she'd have to find another job. "We don't want no trouble."

"I know. And there won't be any."

"Promise?"

"I just want to see what goes on in a place like this."

"You promise?"

Daily smiled. The girl was sweet in her dopey way. "Promise."

The girl pushed a ticket across. Daily paid her and went inside.

The stench was awful. She didn't have to wonder what it was. The stench of lonely, desperate futile sex. No one to be tender with afterward. Just release, and then loneliness again.

Pendrake had disappeared inside, where a film was playing on the screen. Daily could see the image of a woman pleasing herself and writhing about through the gauzy curtain over the entrance alcove.

She parted the curtains and started down the sloping aisle.

She took a seat rows behind Pendrake and ducked down in case he turned around to look at her. But he didn't.

All the perverts finally settled down and went back to exploring themselves or whatever it was they'd been doing.

The rest of the film took twenty minutes.

Daily kept laughing. And every time she laughed, one of the perverts would glare at her. It was sort of like listening to a hellfire-and-brimstone sermon and laughing every third line or so. The faithful didn't appreciate it.

Most of the film seemed to center around the fact that this really ugly guy with a lot of tattoos and blackheads was very well endowed. Daily wouldn't know. She was a real naive person in some ways and hoped to stay that way. Every time one of the blowsy women would tell the sleazy guy on the screen how well endowed he was, he'd chuckle and say, "Yeah, I really am, ain't I, babe?"

At which point Daily would start tittering again, because the guy was such a weenie it was unbelievable. And he thought he was so cool, so cool.

And then, finally, at great interminable length, it was over.

The house lights came up.

Daily slumped down in her seat so Pendrake wouldn't notice her.

The theater reeked.

She felt nauseated.

What the hell was she doing here, anyway?

"And now, gentlemen—and lady—the moment we've all been waiting for."

The speaker was this dumpy little guy in a spangly tuxedo jacket, white shirt, black trousers, and badly scuffed black shoes. Most of the spangles had fallen

off the jacket. The guy had jowls and beady eyes and
a limp and even from here you could see how hard he
was sweating. He was shabby and sad, like everything else in this place, and Daily just wanted to *get
the hell out of there*.

"Do I need to remind you of what thrills await you
tonight?"

The perverts sort of grumbled, no, huh-uh, the guy
didn't need to remind them.

"So without further ado, *the Mynd Girl*!"

Daily was glad they'd turned down the lights
again. The theater—all water-stained and cracked
walls, ripped-up seats and smoke-hazed air—was
better displayed in a faint, dusky light.

The Mynd-Girl came out onstage to a drumroll and
immediately went into a bump-and-grind routine.

She'd done maybe fifty gyrations, including aiming her pelvis directly at the yelling, shouting, foot-
stamping perverts several times, before Daily
noticed that the woman, who looked like a forty-
year-old Terran matron who just happened to have
blue-hued skin, was deformed.

She was missing her left arm.

The Mynd-Girl was obviously used to not having
an arm by now. She threw her feather boa around
with no trouble, she rubbed her crotch with rough
enthusiasm, and she blew kisses with the skill of a
duchess being nice to poor people.

And then the Mynd-Girl started aiming her mind,
not just her pelvis, at the men.

One by one, they'd jump up in their seats and let
out a whoop that was both amusing and a little
frightening.

The Mynd-Girl had made her connection.

All the men were going into ecstacy.

There was an explanation for all this, where
Mynd-Girls came from, how Mynd-Girls functioned
as low-level telepaths, what men felt when a Mynd-

Girl tapped into their sexual fantasies, but Daily had never been interested enough to pay attention.

One man got so excited that he started rushing the stage, his intent clear, but the limping emcee with the spangly jacket tripped him, and then brought a bottle down over the back of his skull.

Another man stood up and started crying, wailing, screaming. Maybe this was the ultimate ecstasy, when you completely lost control.

Then she noticed Pendrake.

He sat in his seat unmoving, staring directly at the stage.

The Mynd-Girl was just now noticing him, and when she did, she stopped.

Right in the middle of her act.

The erotic music still thumping the air.

The perverts still yelling and throwing themselves around and publicly abusing themselves.

And Daily sinking even farther into her chair, totally embarrassed by this whole thing.

Something happened but Daily wasn't sure what.

The Mynd-Girl, almost trancelike, walked to the apron of the stage and looked down at Pendrake.

And then the lights went out, the whole theater so dark Daily couldn't see anything.

And this time when the cry came, presumably a cry of ecstacy, it wasn't a male sound at all.

It was female.

And it was coming from the stage, the unmistakable wail of a woman reaching her sexual zenith. Daily felt embarrassed for everybody in the theater, including herself. Now she was sort of glad that the lights weren't on. *Hearing* all this was bad enough. Seeing it would have pushed Daily over the edge.

Daily could hear the emcee moving around up onstage, cursing, shouting for the lights to be brought up.

The perverts were no longer in ecstacy.

They were angry, booing and stamping their feet, wanting to return to the nice warm wombs the Mynd-Girl had covered them with.

The lights came on.

The Mynd-Girl was back at her act, picking up the beat. The perverts started whistling again.

Daily looked down the aisle to where Pendrake was sitting. Or was supposed to be sitting.

He was gone.

Sometime while the lights were out, he'd vanished.

Chapter Seventeen

Kettering got to flash his badge three times in less than an hour. This was a record for the young cop. Usually, he didn't get off the precinct ship at all, and when he did he was in uniform, so there wasn't much need to show his badge. But tonight, all duded up like a cowhand, he had to flash his badge at all three flier rental shops he stopped at.

Unfortunately, that was the only thing going Kettering's way. None of the three people he talked to knew anything about a small man with a black mustache in a black suit. Nor did they know anything about a convertible flier. Business was slow, they said, real slow, and so there hadn't been any flier rentals for the past four days.

Now Kettering was entering store number four, and playing star cop wasn't as much fun as it had been two humid, sweaty, mosquito-infested hours ago. Now it wasn't even a lot of fun to show his badge.

He went over to the counter, to a fleshy man in a T-shirt that read: I DON'T ANSWER COMPLAINTS. The man looked up, saw the badge Kettering held out to him, and frowned. "Oh, great, just what I fuckin' need."

And a good, good evening to you, sir, Kettering thought, remembering his Academy training. Always better, said the instructors at the Academy, to smile than frown. Better for your facial muscles.

But right now Kettering didn't care about his facial muscles. He just wanted to tell this guy that he,

Kettering, wasn't exactly having a wonderful evening, either.

"So what is it?"

"I'm working on a murder investigation."

"And I'm supposed to be impressed? You think I don't got shit of my own to do?"

S-m-i-l-e. "Have you rented any fliers in the last forty-eight hours?"

"So what if I did? Is that against the law or something?"

"We're looking for a small man with dark hair and a dark mustache."

Recognition showed in the man's mean little eyes. "That guy, huh? I figured something was wrong with him."

"Why's that?"

"Why's that? Shit, he barely spoke. Just nodded. Or shook his head. Weird. You know?"

"When did he rent the flier?"

"Last night about this time."

"When did he bring it in?"

The guy held up a finger, took two steps to the right, and punched up a computer.

While the guy waited for his information, Kettering looked around.

At first glance, the place seemed well taken care of. There were lines of fliers and other vehicles used for recreation. There were cubbyhole offices along one wall where salespeople took customers when they wanted to finalize their deals. And there were big tri-D vid screens where customers could put themselves right into the picture and have the experience of driving whatever vehicle they were looking at.

The guy needed to spend a little money on cooling the place. The air was sticky and sluggish. Oil from the garage in back lay thick and pungent on the air. And the guy himself could do with a bath.

"Not in."

"What?" Kettering said, moving down the counter to where the computer was.

"Hasn't brought it back yet. Good thing you came in, after all. I'm gonna report the son of a bitch stolen."

"Before you do that, let me put an APB out on the flier and the guy in the mustache."

"What the hell's that?"

"APB? All-points bulletin."

"Oh, yeah, like on the vid cop shows."

"Yes, sort of, anyway."

"They're all bullshit, aren't they?"

"The shows?"

"Yeah."

Kettering shrugged. "Not completely."

"Aw, hell." The chunky guy laughed. "All that runnin' and fightin' and shootin'. Shit, you guys wouldn't know what to do if that stuff happened to you. One of my ex-brother-in-laws was a star cop, and he told me you guys don't do squat, just sit up in that precinct ship and play with yourselves."

"That's what he said, huh?"

The fat guy grinned. "That's what he said."

"Well, you can tell your ex-brother-in-law that I say he's full of shit. You got that?"

The chunky guy saw that Kettering was in no mood for any more jollity. The chunky guy started noticing how Kettering's biceps filled out the cowboy shirt and how wide the kid's hands were and how mean those green eyes suddenly looked.

"You want the license number for that flier?" the guy said.

"Yeah."

"Hey, I didn't mean to piss ya off."

"Just give me the goddamn license number."

So that's just what the chunky guy did, just gave Kettering the goddamn license number.

· · ·

Captain Carnes had gas.

This was not an uncommon state of affairs, nor was it one for levity, at least not in front of the good captain.

Carnes had little humor to begin with; he had absolutely none where his gastrointestinal problems were concerned.

Now he sat behind a locked door, one foot up on the desk, relieving himself whenever it was necessary and listening to the official tape of the whole St. Romaine murder.

This was the role Carnes frequently played in homicides. He sat up here inside the belly of the 107th living it out with his gas problems, and listening again and again to the information various cops and various computers had put together for him.

He had solved any number of cases this way.

He might be a little bit too resplendent in the paunch to run much; he might be a little rusty to be much good with a gun; and he might be a little too full of himself to be a very good interrogator but by God he was a good listener.

And when cops listened, really *listened*, they learned things.

So Carnes, with his gas problems and his headphones, sat there and listened.

And then abruptly stopped the tape.

And abruptly played back the last few minutes.

He'd been listening to a background check on Dirk St. Romaine's personal secretary, Mr. Pendrake, when something struck him as curious.

Or wrong.

Or both curious *and* wrong.

Whatever, somewhere on that part of the tape he'd just listened to what was some kind of clue.

So he listened again.

And again.

This section of tape had been supplied by a Federation computer that dealt with the complete life histories of all the suspects who'd ever received Federation welfare help, which Pendrake had gotten when he was a teenager.

Carnes wondered why.

And so when he started listening to the tape, this section came along and . . .

There. He heard it again, somewhere in the three-minute description of the planets where young Pendrake had lived as an orphan—Centurius, Xenon, Calibrite, Tsarik. . . .

Carnes kept trying to figure out why this list sounded so important to him.

Something about one of the planets named?

But they were all nowhere worlds.

Absolutely nowhere.

And the gas started rumbling through his stomach again and for a long time he couldn't think of anything, especially not some list of unimportant planets.

All he could do was sit there and suffer.

Oh my God, how he suffered.

All this happened after Lyra returned from the (she'd actually tittered saying the phrase) "powder room."

Here were Obo and Lyra sitting at a nice, cozy little table in the middle of the nightclub where Ahmed, the Master Mentalist, was soon to perform— and then all of a sudden a harsh white stream of light encircled them and a hearty, unseen male said, "Ladies and gentlemen of The Campfire Room, we have a very special treat to announce tonight."

At this point, Lyra leaned over and squeezed Obo's hand. She was grinning coyly. Then, as an afterthought, she took her napkin, leaned over once again, and buffed the shiny star cop badge she'd made him wear on his chest.

"See this big green fella right here?" the oily male voice went on. "Well, guess what he is, folks! He's a"—he paused for dramatic effect here—"star cop! It's our pleasure to be sharing our dinner with a star cop! Isn't that just great!"

Since nobody else seemed to be getting the idea, Lyra herself sprang to her feet and led the standing ovation.

My God, Obo thought, not only is she a groupie, she's also a cheerleader.

By the end of the standing ovation, Lyra had even managed to manufacture a few tears, which sparkled as they rolled down her nice cheeks, leaving a silver and theatrical trail.

And then, thank God, it was over.

Obo sat down. Even though he was in a bad mood, he hummed "Buckaroo" under his breath.

The spotlight went off.

The announcer went away to announcer heaven.

The other patrons went back to eating their dinners.

And Obo sat—sort of stunned, really—feeling used and confused and kind of sorry for himself.

"I'll never forget this night," Lyra whispered romantically.

"Neither will I," Obo said, though with a great deal less romance in his voice.

He wanted to sulk for a while but the food in front of him looked awful darned good. And from experience he knew that it was difficult to sulk and eat at the same time so he made a quick choice in favor of eating, and plowed in.

Taus were known to be nice, neighborly folks, no doubt, but they had one little social failing: if they weren't careful—very, very careful—they could eat like hogs. Grunt, grunt, grunt, slurp, slurp, slurp, till those nearby wanted to cover their ears and run shrieking from the room.

Ordinarily, Obo would have been very careful of his table manners, particularly when he was with a woman as lovely as Lyra. But, given the way she'd used him as a trophy tonight, he felt that he didn't have to worry about table manners, and ate the way he normally ate.

At first, she looked over at him as if she were hearing things. Nobody could possibly make that much noise when he ate. Then she noticed how the other diners around them had also started looking at Obo.

My God.

Then she noticed how the maître d', far in the back of the big room, began pointing to the front, where Obo sat shoveling food in with all the abandon of a crazed steam shovel.

Grunt, grunt, grunt; slurp, slurp, slurp.

My God.

And then he was done.

Just like that.

Leaning back in his chair and daubing his napkin to his mouth with surprising grace.

Fortunately for everybody else, the Taus were not only the noisiest eaters in the Federation, they were also the fastest.

Before Lyra could say anything, or even think anything else really, a drumroll sounded from somewhere, and a circle of spotlight, very much like the one that had encircled Obo, shone down on the stage.

The same greasy-voiced announcer who had swooned over Obo now swooned over Ahmed.

"Ladies and gentlemen, it is with extreme pride, with extreme pleasure, with extreme good fortune, that The Campfire Room gives that all-seeing, all-knowing, all-powerful seer of other realms . . . Ahmed, the Master Mentalist."

But instead of Ahmed, Obo saw this really gorgeous redhead wearing sexy seamed black hose and a tiny little costume that made the word "revealing" an understatement.

"And now," the male disembodied voice went on, "Ahmed's assistant, the beautiful Shana, will help materialize Ahmed right before your very eyes."

Shana flicked her long, lovely fingers.

A smoke bomb exploded.

From the center of the red smoke, all got up like a swami, emerged (you guessed it) the Master Mentalist himself.

He took a long and very dramatic bow, though Obo wasn't sure why, seeing that the guy hadn't actually done anything yet.

And then Ahmed went into his act.

It was pretty pathetic, actually. Rabbits out of a hat? Cooing pigeons out of a huge silk scarf? Going into the audience and guessing which older women had children at home (most of them, of course)? Shana holding up a card and The Master Mentalist guessing which card she held, even though he was blindfolded?

Pretty pathetic was right, and one could tell by the restlessness of the crowd that they agreed.

L-a-m-e was the proper word here.

Hell, he wasn't even a mentalist, except for a couple of predictions he made while feeling up this crummy little crystal ball that the beautiful Shana held for him. His predictions were: "Mankind will someday once again know war, alas" and "Somewhere in the Federation someday, there will be a great natural disaster."

Gee, thanks for all that useful info, Your Swamiship.

But just as the Master Mentalist was starting to lose the crowd completely—table conversations had started up again, *loud* table conversations—there was another drumroll, which at least got everybody's attention, and then a really grotesque prop was wheeled onstage by Shana, who deserved a lot better than this.

It was a long box with one hole at one end, and two holes at the other. And Shana was holding up a saw.

The people started grumbling again.

Rabbits out of a hat? Pigeons out of yellow silk scarfs? And now the old saw-somebody-in-half routine?

My God, Ahmed was the worst Master Mentalist in the entire Federation.

But there was one little variation that made this particular trick interesting.

Shana held an electric saw.

And the long box was red with blood.

And it was not Shana who was getting into the box to be sawed in half, it was the Master Mentalist himself.

Reluctantly, the audience, Obo and Lyra included, let themselves be drawn back into the stage act.

Shana, who had a wonderful speaking voice to go along with all her other wonderful parts, said, "As you can see, this feat of magic doesn't always work. The blood of many innocents has been spilled on this box." And she swept her graceful hand in an arc past all the bloodstains. "Which is why Ahmed, the Master Mentalist, now insists that he alone risk the electric saw. He wants no more blood spilled, and if it must be spilled, then he wants it to be his own."

What a guy, that Master Mentalist fella.

But then Shana got very serious and grim.

She pulled the cord on the old-fashioned hand-held electric saw.

The whining, whirring noise had a certain obscene power.

No doubt that it could cut right through the box.

No doubt that it could cut right through flesh and bone.

A woman in the audience screamed in the darkness.

The beautiful Shana raised the small, roaring saw high for everybody to see.

Ahmed, the Master Mentalist, began making hokey fright faces, as if he'd suddenly realized he was caught in the grip of a madwoman.

His legs and feet wriggled desperately.

Shana smiled at the audience, and said into a microphone discreetly tucked into the top of her low-cut *bustier*, "Haven't you always wanted to have your boss in this position?"

The audience applauded, and Shana laughed.

They were really starting to appreciate the act.

The Master Mentalist wriggled his legs and feet some more.

He was really scared. Uh-huh.

And then Shana, her gorgeous, dark eyes glinting evilly, started to bend toward the long, casketlike box of wood.

"Please be gentle with me!" Ahmed cried out.

The crowd loved it.

And then something happened. Obo was the only one who picked it up, possibly because Taus are a particularly sensitive people.

For just a moment, Shana stared at the back of the large, dark nightclub. Obo had no idea what she saw but it was something that disturbed her because suddenly her expression changed. He saw her expression go from one of merriment and theatrical evil to one of . . . what?

He couldn't characterize it. All he knew was that she didn't look right.

In that curious moment when she'd glanced to the back of the club, something had happened.

Obo had a terrible sense of what was about to take place. It would probably be too much to call it a real premonition but it was something very much like that.

Obo jumped to his feet, nearly knocking the table over as he went running toward the front of the club and the stage.

People in the audience must have thought Obo was part of the act because they started laughing and applauding.

And then Shana did it.

And there wasn't time for Obo to stop her.

She bent over, the electric saw crying with power, and started cutting through the box.

It was only seconds before Ahmed, the Master Mentalist, started screaming.

The audience members, insensitive drunken boobs that they were, just laughed and applauded all the louder, right over the Master Mentalist's screams.

Before Obo could reach her and grab her wrist and hurl the power saw across the stage, there was time for the box—and the Master Mentalist as well—to be cut in two halves, and blood and innards began falling to the floor.

Now the audience was screaming. They knew this was no trick.

The Master Mentalist's legs, in some kind of death throes, continued to kick for a few seconds, but then they were still.

The house lights had come up. Everything looked small and shabby, all the magic fled.

Obo stood there, holding Shana by the wrist.

But he needn't have worried. She wasn't going anywhere. A glance at her lovely eyes told him that she was in some kind of deep trance.

The floor was a slippery mess. Obo had to be careful not to slide or trip as he led the beautiful woman off the stage and into the back of the night-club.

Behind him, still onstage, he saw a small man in a tuxedo bending over and vomiting voluminously.

Obo sort of felt like doing the same thing, actually.

Chapter Eighteen

Brackett hadn't danced in a long time.

He liked the way her flesh felt soft and womanly in his arms, the way her neck and silken dark hair smelled of perfume, the tender thoughts she inspired, even if he was at least slightly afraid of such notions.

They were on a balcony overlooking the river. They'd been dancing for nearly an hour. The stars looked down bright and approving. A breeze off the river was like a kiss of warm night. Probably there were other people around them but he didn't know for sure.

And then the orchestra took a break.

He walked Marcia Tenhold back to their table and as they sat there, a waiter appeared and poured them more champagne.

She raised her sparkling glass and he soon raised his. This was somewhere in the vicinity of the three hundredth toast tonight. But he didn't care. All he noticed was how sweet and pretty she looked in the glow of the candle.

She wasn't a beauty but she had good clean looks and her smile devastated him, being one part loneliness and one part glee.

"Can I say the same old thing again?" She laughed. She was slightly drunk. "I can't think of anything else."

"Be my guest."

She touched her glass to his. " 'I can't think of

when I've had a better time.' God, how many times have I said that tonight?"

"Eighty or ninety."

"That's what I figured." Then she reached across the table and touched his hand. "But it's true, Brackett. After my father died . . ."

Then she stopped, as if realizing that she was being selfish. She wasn't the only one here who'd suffered a loss.

How about Brackett and his wife?

"I know what you're saying," Brackett said quietly. "I feel the same way."

The waiter was back. More champagne. Brackett held up his hand. No more. There was a little case of murder he was supposed to be investigating. He'd take her back to her room and then get back to work.

She watched him over the pulse of the candlelight. "You're back to being Lieutenant Brackett again, aren't you?"

"How could you tell that?"

"Your eyes. They're hard again, the way they were when we first met."

"I'm sorry."

She shrugged. "It's all right." She sounded wistful. "Things this good never last very long anyway." She stared at him across the glow and said, "Maybe that's why they're so sacred—because perfection only comes in little fits and starts."

"I could always find you again, after I'm back on the 107th, I mean."

"It's nice to think so."

"You don't sound very optimistic."

"You know how it goes. People make all sorts of promises to each other."

The orchestra was back.

The maestro struck a downbeat.

"One more dance?" Brackett said.

"Love to."

So they had one more dance all their own in their very special place over by the edge of the balcony overlooking the dark, star-lit water.

He closed his eyes and enjoyed her perfume again.

He held her tighter, yet with great delicacy, too, as if afraid he'd hurt her.

And then he thought of his dead wife and wondered if he had any business at all doing something like this, being with someone like Marcia Tenhold.

"Are you all right?" she said.

"Yes."

"I'm losing you, aren't I?"

"I'm sorry."

She stood on her tiptoes and kissed him tenderly on the mouth. "We should leave before we spoil any memories."

A few moments later, they were walking out the door, into the fresh night air, back toward their hotel, toward the moon so huge on the horizon.

Daily opened the door to her hotel room and found a man in there.

"Oh, God," she said. "I really don't need this right now. I really don't. The guy I was tailing just got away from me and I just saw a Mynd-Girl have some sort of mental orgasm and I need a shower and—"

And then Dreesen brought the fresh-cut flowers from behind his back and Daily couldn't help herself, she burst into tears. Maybe Dreesen was a pain in the ass but he was also, unfortunately for her, a very sweet man.

"Oh, God, Dreesen," she said, "why can't you be a prick like most other men?"

Dreesen looked thoroughly confused.

Chapter Nineteen

Daily wished that she could just close her eyes and when she opened them again, Dreesen would be gone.

God, she liked him and felt so sorry for him . . . but God, she didn't love him.

She sat in her hotel room now, the red roses he'd just brought already in a milk glass vase.

He sat across from her, watching her.

"So you like roses?"

"Right," she said. "I like roses."

This was the third time in less than five minutes he'd asked if she liked roses. This was also the third time in less than five minutes that she said yes, she *did* like roses.

"That's kind of a coincidence."

"Oh?"

"Yeah, my mom likes roses, too."

"Don't most moms like roses?" Daily said, unable to keep a subtle sarcasm from her tone.

"Oh," Dreesen said, "I don't think all moms do."

"But most?"

Dreesen shrugged. "Most but not all."

Oh, God, how much longer could she carry on this conversation?

She knew what he wanted.

He wanted bed and then in the darkness he wanted her pledge of eternal love.

"I can smell them from over here."

Her mind had been wandering. "Pardon."

"The roses."

"The roses?"

"Yes, I was saying I could smell them all the way over here."

"Oh."

"All the way across the room."

"Ah."

"There's nothing as sweet as a rose."

"I imagine not."

"Daily," he began.

"Please don't say it?"

"Pardon?"

"Please don't say it, Dreesen."

"Please don't say what?"

"Whatever you were going to say."

"How did you know what I was going to say?"

"I could just tell. Watching you sit there, I mean. Body language, I guess."

He grinned. "God, I'm sorry I'm so obvious."

"You should think it over some more."

"I don't have to think it over, Daily. I've already made up my mind."

Please don't ask me to marry you, Dreesen.

"I've really got to go to the bathroom, Daily. Sorry to be so rude."

And with that, he was up out of his chair and across the room and in the bathroom with the door closed behind him.

He didn't want to ask me to marry him. He wanted to go to the bathroom.

She was losing it.

All this stress.

It had been such a simple, uncomplicated relationship at the first but now . . .

When he came out, he was smiling. He went over

and sat down and looked directly at her and said, "I've checked with the captain, Daily. We could get married as soon as next week."

"You checked with the captain? You told him about us?"

"I just said we were considering it."

"*You're* considering it, Dreesen. I'm not. I mean . . . I don't want to hurt your feelings, but—"

He held up a hand as if to stop her conversation.

"My mom tells me she was the same way."

"The same way?"

"Sure. When my dad asked her to get married. Said she was scared pea green."

"Pea green?"

"That's an expression of hers."

"But I don't want—I mean, I've never even considered—"

He held up his hand again. "She said that's how you'd respond."

"She did?"

He nodded and grinned boyishly. "It was her idea to bring you the roses. You'll like her."

"Your mom?"

"Right. And my dad, too, for that matter. And they'll like you, too. I figure we can spend part of our honeymoon with them and—"

And then, just as Daily felt deserted, adrift here with this suddenly very self-confident and totally crazy Dreesen, the gods proved their existence when the red alert node implanted in their ears exploded with a small but unmistakable sound.

"An alert!" Daily said, leaping up from the couch. "We've got to go!"

Never had she been more thankful for being summoned.

By the time Dreesen was on his feet, she was at the door.

"But you didn't give me your answer!" he cried.

"I'll meet you at the elevator!" Daily said, and took off running.

Oh, thank you, God.

Thank you.

Chapter Twenty

"You could always stay the night."

"I suppose I could."

"Don't you want to?"

"I suppose I do."

"Now there's real passion."

Brackett smiled. "It's been a while for me. I might be a little awkward."

They stood on the veranda of her hotel room overlooking Tumbleweed City. Below, everything was neon and deep shadow and moonlight.

Brackett sighed.

He understood what he was going through, of course.

Guilt.

Ever since the death of his wife, he'd been walking around with the feeling that the wrong person had been killed.

She'd been the good person, he the bad.

He should have died, not her.

"May I ask you a question?" Marcia Tenhold said.

"Sure."

"Is it your wife?"

"My wife?"

"That you were thinking about then. There was a great sadness in your eyes."

"You're very observant."

"I'm really touched by how much you loved her."

"She was easy to love. I don't know why she had

anything to do with me. Given the sort of man I am, I mean."

"Was."

"Was?"

"You've changed. You used to be a criminal. Now you're a cop."

"Sometimes I wonder if people ever really change," Brackett said, sighing again and looking out at the lights of Tumbleweed City.

She slid her hand in his. It was as frail and sweet as a child's. "I wouldn't care if we made love or not, Brackett. It would just be nice to sleep with you."

He started to turn to her, desire suddenly overcoming his thoughts of Elizabeth, when the red alert node implanted in the bone of his ear sounded.

"Oh," Brackett said, "shit."

"What is it?"

"Red alert."

"Bad."

"Could be." He shrugged. "Probably is."

"You have to leave?"

"I'm afraid so."

"You don't even have time for this?"

At which point she gave Brackett one of the most dizzying kisses of his life.

Three minutes later, he was in the elevator, being hurled seventy-six floors to street level.

Five minutes after that, he was making his quick, sweaty way through the milling crowds blocking the sidewalks in front of the casinos.

It was the usual crowd: a man slapping a woman, a tourist blissed out on some kind of narcotic, a drunk who'd gotten lucky at the slots trying to feel up all three hookers draped over his arms.

Tumbleweed City was not in danger of becoming Brackett's favorite place.

Chapter Twenty-one

By this time, Lieutenant John Paul Johansen was pretty sure he knew the name of the killer. By this time it was a matter of simple deduction.

Each person who was in the murder room had been scanned by the crime-lab people on the scene.

The mysterious sparkling dust (known in computerese as ARC-1750) was found in any significant amounts on only two people, a man named Pendrake and the victim, Dirk St. Romaine. The dust in the air had triggered Carver's violent allergic reaction.

Therefore, a reasonable man would conclude that the name of the killer was Matthew Pendrake.

John Paul Johansen started whistling the magnificent tune that accompanied the acceptance of the Moskowitz.

Then he started punching communicator buttons.

He needed to have a red-alert conference with Carnes, Brackett, Daily, and Obo, summoning each of them to a central point through the red-alert system.

Fifteen minutes later, each star cop occupied a quarter of Johansen's screen.

Johansen began by explaining the origin of the dust, and by assuring them that young Carver would likely be all right now that the dust had been identified, and now that the medicos could treat it better.

He then explained the curious history of the planet Xenon, from which the dust had come, especially the

saga of the facility there that had spawned telepaths.

At which point, Daily said, "That's it! That's why I
got such a headache! And that's who turned the
lights out tonight at the Mynd-Girl's show!"

"If you don't mind, Daily," John Paul Johansen
said in his somewhat stuffy manner, "I'd like to conclude my remarks."

"Oh, sorry, sir."

Johansen continued. He discussed how the dust
had been found in significant amounts on only two
people who were in the room, namely a man named
Pendrake and namely a man called St. Romaine. It
was possible that the killer was a third party, a man
so covered with the dust that it had somehow gotten
all over Pendrake. But that possibility was remote. If
there was so much dust in the room that it had gotten all over Pendrake, then why not all over the star
cops, who, in fact, had been in the room much longer
than Pendrake?

And then he returned to the subject of telepathy,
explaining how telepaths were known to return every few years to Xenon to replenish their powers via
a system Federation scientists understood only im-
perfectly. But this was the likely scenario: Pendrake
had lately made a quick trip to the planet and had
come here right after, carrying the glittering dust.

Then John Paul Johansen smiled the smug smile
for which he was justly known. "A rather wonderful
piece of forensic work, if I do say so myself."

But the star cops were familiar with Johansen's
high opinion of himself and began talking among
themselves, as if Johansen weren't there. The four
quarters of the screen got a lot livelier.

"Then that explains what happened to the beautiful Shana tonight," Obo said. "Pendrake must have
been in the audience and forced her to kill Ahmed."
Then he paused a moment. "But somebody told me

they saw a man dressed in black in Ahmed's room to-day. Who could that have been?"

"Pendrake," Jennifer Daily said, remembering now the man's closet. "He had an entire black costume in his room when I was there, including wig and mustache."

A new face appeared on the screen, momentarily displacing Carnes. The other cops recognized him as the ever-eager and overeager recruit named Kettering.

"Excuse me for interrupting, but I was told this linkup was going on so I thought I'd tell you what I found out."

Kettering then told them about Bagdar coming in and talking about seeing the killer dressed in black take off on a flier from the murder scene. Then he smiled a smile so self-satisfied even John Paul Johansen would envy it.

"So I started checking out all the places that rent fliers and I found a place where the owner identified the guy dressed all in black as renting a flier the night before. The vehicle still hadn't been turned in and was late. We found it an hour ago, ditched in an alley behind the casino."

"Pendrake," Brackett said.

Kettering was suddenly displaced, Captain Carnes reappearing. "Thank you, Kettering," he said.

"I don't have to tell you how dangerous Pendrake is," Carnes said to the three cops. "I also don't have to tell you that I want him brought in immediately. Lieutenant Johansen, can you tell us anything about the abilities of these telepaths?"

Johansen, back on screen, beamed. He was pleased to be the center of attention again. Star cops were mere functionaries; forensic scientists were the real white-hats.

"From the reports I read, each telepath varied widely in abilities. But it is safe to assume, from what he's done thus far, that he can effect at least a crude kind of mind control. Look what he did to Shana tonight. On the other hand, it's unlikely that he can kill with his mind. If he could, he probably wouldn't have been so pedestrian in the way he murdered St. Romaine. But, as Captain Carnes said, he's obviously still very, very dangerous. While his powers won't work on everybody—some people can resist ESP suggestion just the way others can resist hypnotic suggestion—you may not find out your own abilities to resist him until it's too late. I'd be very, very careful."

Carnes came back on in Johansen's place. "I'm putting out a general order for his arrest. I want each of you three officers to begin looking for him right away."

Brackett nodded, "You'll cover the space ports?"

"Of course." Carnes saluted them. "Good luck."

They saluted him in return, expecting the line to go dead.

But once again Johansen was in Carnes's square. "Pretty good work, don't you think?"

Brackett wanted to say something sarcastic but even he had to admit that the braggart Johansen really did have good reason to brag this time.

"You'll probably win a Moskowitz for this," Brackett said.

Johansen played it coy as he could. "A Moskowitz? Me? God, I never even thought of that."

"No," Brackett said sarcastically. "No, it probably never even crossed your mind."

At which, the three star cops punched themselves from the screen with buttons on their own communicators, leaving Johansen all alone to keep on babbling about how perfectly wonderful he was.

The three star cops got right to work.

Chapter Twenty-two

At one point in his life, Matthew Pendrake had considered the possibility that he would someday be God. Oh, not the one and only God (if such a thing existed) to be sure, but God when compared to his fellow mortals, those who neither possessed nor understood telepathic powers to equal his.

Throughout the Federation, the subculture that had grown up around the far-flung telepaths whispered constantly about Matthew Pendrake and how he would someday be the most powerful of them all.

He was, it was even conjectured, the next step in the evolution of telepaths.

Much of this talk was due to the fact that on the world called Andor, he had been attacked by a lumbering, armored, and quite deadly beast called by natives the Monster of the Muck, due to the fact that the beast enjoyed nothing so much as rolling around in drying rivers and coating himself the color of the soil.

But when the beast attacked, it was startled to see the young man known as Matthew Pendrake holding his ground.

Simply standing there, calmly, waiting for the beast to draw closer, closer.

And then Matthew Pendrake put forth his right hand and from it, all invisible, shot beams of psychic powers that had heretofore been thought impossible.

First, the beast lost its left eye, exploding blood and tissue, and then its right eye. And then a long, running rent appeared in its throat, spewing blood like a geyser. And then its very head split down the middle, spilling out brain matter, which splashed steaming hot to the ground. And then his midsection was opened up, and as its armor was painfully peeled back (the dying noises the beast made were sad and desperate beyond belief) like huge, gnarled scabs, the thin shimmering membrane covering its innards was revealed.

And then of course the beast was dead.

And within days the story was whispered throughout the Federation.

Matthew Pendrake. The first of a new breed, a mutant breed, perhaps, a breed that would set telepaths on the proper course to power throughout the federated worlds.

At the time, Matthew Pendrake had been nineteen years old.

He spent the next two years of his life roaming the worlds and enjoying himself. If there was a jewel he wanted or needed, he took it simply by convincing the owner to give it to him. And just so did he take the bodies of fabulous women, a benumbing succession of them on a whirligig tour of the planets.

Thinking that he had his entire life for more purposeful endeavors, Pendrake continued his self-indulgent life.

He might have sought out great scientific secrets, yet he preferred furtive sex.

He might have tried to communicate with species that the scientific community had found only mute, but he preferred the excitement of bars just at melancholy dusk.

He might have spent time with telepaths less gifted than himself, trying to enhance their powers and thus further their cause, but he chose instead whatever drug was fashionable at the moment.

And then one day he awoke on a strange world, in

a strange hotel room, nauseated from three continu-
ous weeks of pleasure, and found that most of his
powers were gone.

From the beginning, telepaths had known that
their powers diminished as they grew older. An
eight-year-old telepath was generally far more gifted
than a forty-year-old.

But it was felt that, given his extraordinary tal-
ents, Matthew Pendrake did not have to worry about
losing his abilities.

But gone they were, and soon enough Pendrake
drifted from resort planet to resort planet, winning
enough at gambling (telepathy came in very handy
at poker tables) to support himself but not enough to
attract attention.

He had been unmanned. He was no longer mutant
king; he was just another drab scuttling human being with a few powers scarcely worth mentioning.

And then one day he met Dirk St. Romaine and
they began talking and Pendrake saw a way that his
remaining powers could be used to great novel
consequence—he could read the minds of celebrities
and pass along his knowledge to Dirk St. Romaine.

And together they would get rich.

And together they would tour the federated
worlds, life-of-the-party.

And together they would expose one vid star after
another as the sleazy trashoid he/she really was.

But what he hadn't counted on was Dirk St. Romaine's ego, never paying Pendrake sufficiently,
never treating him like anything more than a servant.

And then one night, Pendrake couldn't take any
more and he killed him.

Like that; just like that.

And now he stood watching the vid as his face
flashed on the screen and the announcer said that the

star cops wanted Matthew Pendrake for questioning in the murder of Dirk St. Romaine.

And then, almost without realizing it, he started to walk, and then started to jog, and then started to run.

Down the rain-sparkling neon streets of the casino section.

Running faster now; faster.

Faster.

He was a tourist from Arduran, a chubby little man of forty-three who worked in the accounting department of one of the big mining companies out near Vega, and he'd never had a wife nor even a steady girlfriend really, and sometimes living with his mother got so bad, so incredibly oppressive, that he walked through the night streets of his home planet for hours on end, wondering how his life had ever gone by so quickly, wondering if he'd ever get out from under the perfumed shadow of his captor. And, so by God, he'd come to Tumbleweed with enough cash to goggle a Sultan and enough lust to stop the heart of a satyr. He had spent every waking moment of these weeks in the presence of a beautiful lady. So what if they had credit cards for hearts. So what if they laughed a little too quickly and tinnily at his shy jokes. So what if they seemed a little embarrassed when he said, after their brief time in bed, "I love you." The only two living beings he'd ever said that to in his life were his mother and his dog Raffles when it was dying in the street after being struck by a car. It was great, glorious fun to say "I love you," so during his three weeks here, he'd said it as often as he could. *I love you, I love you, I love you.* He thought of all this as he stood next to the flier station one block down from the budget motel where he'd been staying. He was a tidy little man, and a frugal one, and taking a private flier directly from his hotel meant

having to tip the doorman and the flier driver. Better
to take a mass-transit flier. After all, a short walk
was good for the body and soul alike, not to mention,
in this case, good for the pocketbook. No tipping at
all.

He stood alone, lost in his memories (redhead, bru-
nette, golden flowing blonde) of the past three weeks.

So he didn't see the man—sweating and out of
breath—emerge from the alley behind him.

Didn't hear the man—gasping and cursing under
his breath—come up behind him.

Didn't feel the man—harder than necessary, and
in a single quick lunge—shove a blaster into his back
until it was too late.

"I'm perfectly willing to kill you right here," said
the man.

"Oh, my," said the tidy and frugal visitor from
Arduran. "Oh, my."

In the alley, Pendrake slugged the little bastard,
and then proceeded to vandalize his body.

Because they were essentially the same size
(though not the same manner, Pendrake hoped,
thinking of the other man's prim and anxious way),
Pendrake had himself a new set of clothes, a nice
new piece of luggage, a new identi-card, and a
paid-up one-way ticket to Vega.

In less than an hour, he'd be soaring through
space.

To freedom.

In a week or so, he'd be on Artair, where the traffic
was heavy in the contraband art of body sculpting.
He would get himself a brand-new, and permanent,
identity.

Pendrake looked down at the tubby little man, who
looked so ludicrous in his underwear, and noticed
blood trickling down the right side of his head from
the gash the handle of the blaster had made there.

Pendrake almost felt sorry for the little bastard.

Nobody should be that much of a cowering little twerp.

A great feeling of revulsion suddenly filled Pendrake. He detested the little man and everything the little man represented.

Pendrake drew his right foot back and then began savagely kicking the little man in the ribs.

Unconscious, the little man put up no defense.

Pendrake kept his right foot busy until he heard the satisfying crack of bones.

Only then did he stop, sweating again, panting.

He spit on the little man, then watched a silver goober riding the little man's forehead.

Pathetic little creep.

For good measure, Pendrake kicked him one more time.

Then he left the alley and took his rightful place at the flier stand.

Soon enough, he would be at the rocket port and off this world.

Chapter Twenty-three

Daily had been in a 'copter crash once. For six uninterrupted nights afterward, she'd had terrible nightmares of hearing a rotor rip inexplicably from overhead, and then fall, crashing, to the desert floor below. But even though the nightmares faded, Daily never forgot the crash—the sudden sense of terrible free-fall; the voice of the pilot who had lost all semblance of control; and the hard smashing contact with the earth below. And then . . . darkness. And faintly, cold. The chill of death? She'd never been able to quite decide—had she actually been dead a few moments there?—because then there were human voices and the chugging noises of emergency 'copters, and then the cool white feel of hospital sheets. She had survived, even though, sadly, the pilot had not.

This was only her sixth 'copter ride since that accident three years ago.

She still counted every single 'copter ride, as if she would reach some magical number someday and then be all right again. Not start to tremble when she boarded. Not start to sweat when the big metal bird started lifting her upward. Not say a silent little prayer, even though she was pretty much a nonbeliever, when the 'copter started hauling ass.

Please, God. If you exist, that is. Please.

The 'copter was skimming the eight-lane highway leading to the rocket port.

Daily, Brackett, and Obo were packed into the passenger seats. The pilot was really giving the machine the stick as they flew about fifty feet above the gleaming alloy hulks of the colorful turbo cars below them.

This was the part of a manhunt that Brackett hated in particular.

When you were reduced to skimming all the roads leading to the rocket port, looking for anything that appeared suspicious, you had to admit to yourself that you had nothing else to go on.

That, in fact, the suspect and not the star cops, was in control of the situation.

They skimmed this way for ten minutes, desert to one side of the wide highway, foothills, and finally mountains on the other side.

"Look," Obo said.

"Where?" Brackett said.

"That old car. The gray one."

"What about it?" Brackett said.

The 'copter smelled of grease in the hot sunlight. The rotors made enough noise to give Daily a headache.

Behind dark glasses, Brackett narrowed his eyes to squint at the ancient skimmer that had suddenly veered off the highway onto a dusty road leading to desert.

"What the hell's that all about?" Brackett said.

People didn't drive into the desert unless there was some kind of emergency—or unless they had something to hide.

"Hand me the scanner," Daily said.

Obo reached down and picked up a small shotgun-style device from the trembling floor.

Just as Daily started to point the scanner at the skimmer below them, the vehicle stopped in the middle of the vast sandy nowhere.

One man jumped from the driver's side of the car, another man leaped from the other.

Then both of them began running as fast as they could in opposite directions.

"Hurry, Daily!" Brackett said.

Daily fired the scanner, a device that electronically catalogued everything inside the skimmer, in effect an X-ray. The scanner started making a wild whooping noise. Contraband had been discovered. The two men were running to escape the star cops.

And just then the car exploded into a mass of tumbling red flame and black smoke, the men hoping to destroy the evidence.

But it was too late. Daily had all the legal evidence that would be needed right in the scanner.

"Send somebody out here to pick up two druggers," Brackett shouted into his microphone. He then told home base the approximate location and wished them good luck.

"Now let's try and get serious," Brackett said, his voice sounding frustrated, even angry now. "Let's go find Matthew Pendrake."

On a world like Tumbleweed, a manhunt is no easy procedure. For one thing, local law enforcement is not well trained, and for another, the folks who run the casinos and the resorts want to minimize the fact that there's a manhunt going on at all. Why scare off all those wonderful cash-laden tourists who came here for a good time?

So it was that Captain Carnes found himself seriously inhibited when putting the dragnet in place. Local authorities simply wouldn't let him do his job the way he wanted to.

The compromise worked out included the following: all local vid channels broadcast a holo of Matthew Pendrake every five minutes; the entire rocket port facility swarmed with local gendarmes on the

lookout for Pendrake; twenty local cops gathered together to walk through the center of the gambling-
hotel area in a sweep.

Not ideal, not what Captain Carnes wanted at all,
but better than nothing.

The 'copter carrying Brackett, Daily, and Obo set
down at the space port five minutes after the incident in the desert.

Brackett knew that the most likely place for Matthew Pendrake was here, among the crowds
awaiting the departure of one of the rockets that
stood gleaming in the afternoon sunlight.

Somewhere among the gawky, dusty, impatient,
exhausted tourists, they would find their man.

Brackett was sure of it.

The three cops, well armed and eager to confront
their prey, started their own sweep of the multilevel
port, including a search of the twelve-story hotel.

Matthew Pendrake went up to the departure
booth, held up his identi-card, and applied it to the
acknowledgment pad built into the wall.

There was a momentary delay while the computers checked out his new identity—Mr. Roland B.
Hawthorne—and confirmed his reservation on
Flight 233, which was departing in exactly forty-
three minutes and twenty-five seconds. Late depar-
tures were unheard of.

Pendrake sighed and smiled.

How simple life could be sometimes.

Just a short while ago, things had looked terribly
bleak for him.

But now . . .

He decided to go get himself a nice, cool drink and
then wait in the swarming departure area with all
the other tourists.

He found a robot bar called Name Your Poison and
disappeared into the deep shadows inside.

When the three star cops arrived at the space port,
they divided up their duties to make their search
more efficient. Brackett took the bars in the hotel,
Daily took all the departure gates in the terminal
proper, and Obo took the shops and bars and rest
rooms, and anywhere else that might offer a hiding
place to a fugitive.

Manhunts usually produced any number of serio-
comic moments, and this one was no different.

One of the bars Brackett checked out was in the
course of hosting an all-nude birthday bash for a
Terran senator.

On her way to one of the departure gates, Daily
was accosted by members of a religious sect pleading
for money (they always trolled space ports like this
one) and finally had to deck the leader in order to get
away and do her job.

And Obo, in a men's rest room on the off chance
that he'd find Pendrake cowering in here, decided to
wash his dusty hands, but the water came out too
splashing fast and covered his crotch with an un-
seemly amount of water. He had to spend the next fifteen minutes checking out the various shops, bars,
and rest rooms with people glancing at his crotch
and smirking. People loved to see star cops humiliate
themselves. On some planets it was a virtual sport.

Ten minutes after they began their sweep, the
three star cops paused in their efforts, unclipped
their communicators from their uniform belts, and
held a small conference.

"Any sign of him?" Brackett asked Daily.

"Zilch."

"How about you, Obo?"

"Squat."

"Damn," Brackett said. "We'll just have to keep looking."

"Have you considered the fact that he could already have gotten off the planet?" Daily asked.

Which were not exactly the words Brackett longed to hear at this moment.

"Yeah," he said, "I've considered it."

Then he cut off contact and went back to looking for Matthew Pendrake.

Which was just what Daily and Obo did, too.

Her name was Angela Mainwaring and this was her first day on Tumbleweed and she was armed with three years' worth of vacation savings and a horoscope that hinted strongly that she was about to meet "a most attractive man."

She had spent the morning in two different casinos. Gambling was only part of it. What she really liked was walking around inside the vast, glitzy casinos themselves. Every few minutes, it seemed, she saw this or that vid star, most of them, unfortunately, looking pretty hung over from last night's revelry. Another fun thing to do was to take a seat at one of the free-drinks bars and just watch the plain everyday folks like herself wander around and ogle the gold-encrusted ceilings and walls. She liked to watch other people take pleasure in things like this. It only enhanced the pleasure she took in the very same things.

At one point earlier in the day, she'd had a bad moment when she recalled all the miserable love affairs she'd had in the past ten years, working as a lonely secretary at a factory that turned out the knobs that soldiers wore on their deep-space life-support equipment. There had been Ben, Ed, Joe, Bob, Ernest, Hap, Algernon, and Blinky. And probably a few more she'd forgotten about. And they'd all dumped her. All of them. Oh, they each had their own very particular reasons for doing so, but the result was the same: they were gone. Rather than face these bitter memories, Angela had slugged down a few stiff drinks and gone back to the gambling tables. The prospect of losing all her money fixed her mind most wonderfully.

Much later in the day she had decided to walk around the downtown area and "take in some air," as she'd told the boss of the table where she'd just dropped a hefty chunk of her vacation cash. He looked briefly sympathetic, and then turned eagerly back to the fresh suckers.

She was passing an alley when she heard the moan, and when she turned to see the cause of the noise, she saw a naked man staggering to his feet.

Her first impulse was to scream because heroines always did that on the vid; they screamed and screamed and screamed.

So she screamed.

The naked man, still staggering, waved his hands at her and said, "I need you to help me."

She had two thoughts simultaneously.

Her horoscope had said that she would meet a "most attractive man." It had not, however, defined "attractive." True, most people would interpret that to mean that the man would at least remotely resemble one of the hunks who was on the vid all the time. In that, the naked man failed utterly. He was a butterball. No way around it. But he had just uttered, albeit in a weakened condition and perhaps out of his mind, the words she had longed for a man to say to her. "I need you to help me." Because neither Ben nor Ed nor Joe nor Bob nor Ernest nor Hap nor Algernon and certainly not Blinky had ever said anything remotely like this to her. *I need you to help me.*

Her other thought was that the naked man waving his arms was badly hurt. An amoeba-shaped patch of dark blood covered the right side of his head, matting his hair, causing it to glisten.

And so she realized that her horoscope had just come true in the most unlikely circumstances of all.

She had indeed met a "most attractive man." A man who needed her.

Now, as he started to totter again, as he began to pitch forward to the alley, she went to him, bringing succor and sustenance . . . and help.

He fell into her arms and she hugged him with great and abiding love.

The name of the local cop was Ready. He was young, twenty-three, and he had but one dream, which was becoming a bona fide star cop. But three times he had taken the entrance exam and three times he had failed. Not even with implants was his vision good enough to don the uniform he so cherished. So he'd picked one of the motif worlds at random and had settled there as a rent-a-cop for casino management.

Today, he was working the streets, walking up and down the sidewalks seeing if he could be of any service to any of the gaudy tourists.

He had resigned himself, even at this young age, to never playing any role whatsoever in any case of any consequence. He would just smile pretty for the ladies and laugh at the bland tourist jokes of the men.

Then, thirty seconds ago, just as he rounded a corner, he saw a most unlikely sight: two rather overweight people standing in the entrance to an alley. One of them was a woman and a rather overweight one at that, and the other was a man who was of similar size but with one very dramatic difference.

The man was naked. Birthday-suit naked. Jaybird naked.

Ready started running forward, hand to his weapon, to see just what the hell was going on here.

For the first time in his two-year career as a rent-a-cop, Ready felt like something resembling a real police officer.

A naked man in broad daylight in downtown Tumbleweed.

Yea, and the Lord be praised.

Ten seconds later, he reached the curious couple and started firing questions at them.

Just like a cop.

At this same time, Brackett was chasing a man down a long corridor on the third tier of the vast stone building adjacent to the space port. He ultimately caught up with the man after shouting "Stop!" so loud that half the people on the same tier turned around and looked. It was the wrong man.

At this same time, Daily was running up three flights of stairs trying to beat an elevator headed for the fourth floor on the restaurant side of the port. She had seen the elevator doors close on a man who looked just like Matthew Pendrake, except with a dark, droopy mustache. When the elevator doors parted, there stood Daily, out of breath and eager as ever. But when she saw the guy with the dark, droopy mustache, she frowned. It was the wrong man.

At this same time, Obo was in one of the men's rooms, leaning against a sink—his back to the faucets, taking no chances this time—waiting for the stall down the way to open and the man to emerge. Obo had asked one of the port employees if he'd seen a man fitting Matthew Pendrake's description anywhere around. Yeah, as a matter of fact, I think I seen a guy that sounds just like him duck in that men's room about five minutes ago. So Obo had gone in and was waiting. And then the guy came out. Either the port employee was legally blind or he was having some fun at Obo's expense. It was the wrong man.

• • •

It took Ready five excited minutes to get the whole story.

Clearly, Matthew Pendrake had taken the naked man's clothing and identi-card and was now probably on his way out of Tumbleweed's orbit.

Ready got on his communicator and called the star cops pronto.

His message was beamed up to the precinct ship and then straight back down to Brackett.

"Can the man describe his clothes?" Brackett asked Ready.

"Can you describe your clothes?"

The round little man started speaking into the communicator as if he were going to give a speech.

"A one-piece buff blue suit, a blue kerchief with a gold slide band, and a pair of orange suede boots."

The guy was a tourist, all right, Brackett thought. Nobody but a tourist would wear orange suede boots.

"Lieutenant Brackett?" Ready asked when the tourist had finished with his bit.

"Yes?"

"I wonder if we could get together later. I . . . I might need some advice getting into the star cops."

Brackett grinned sadly. Half the rent-a-cops in the Federation wanted to be real live star cops. Many were called, few were chosen.

"When this gets wrapped up, give the precinct ship another call. They'll put us in touch."

"Really?" He was so excited he forgot to say "sir." He hoped Brackett didn't take offense. He hoped Brackett—

"And good work, Ready."

"Really, sir?"

"Damn good work, in fact."

Ready got chills. He really did.

Chapter Twenty-four

With the number of the robbery victim's identi-card, with a description of the robbery victim's clothes, the star cops moved in on the space port. So did all available rent-a-cops.

The manhunt was now about to pay off.

He was in a lounge when he saw the guy's image on the vid, the vid sitting at the end of the bar and casting a warm silvery glow on the faces of the customers.

"This happy Tumbleweed visitor was on his way back to his home planet when fugitive Matthew Pendrake robbed him of his identi-card and his clothes. We urge all citizens, Tumbleweedian and visitor alike, to be on the lookout for a man dressed in—"

And then came a description of the exact clothes that Matthew Pendrake was wearing.

The bar was dark. Species of half a dozen worlds lined the old-fashioned horseshoe-shaped bar.

Pendrake was down near the end of it. He'd been having a drink, waiting the last few minutes before going to his rocket. Before escaping to freedom.

The funny thing was, nobody along the bar turned their eyes on him right away. A minute or so lapsed before they made the connection.

And he had no trouble tapping their minds.

Hey, dat's da guy onna vid dere.
Hey, that's Matthew Pendrake.
Hey, that's the guy the cops are looking for.

Pendrake could see the fleshy bartender, all duded up in fancy Western attire, reach below the bar for a stunner, a weapon that would immobilize Pendrake till the cops arrived.

But Pendrake was having none of it.

He focused his mind on the bartender.

The stunner ripped from the man's hand and went flying into a tray of glasses at the opposite end of the bar.

None of the customers could believe what they'd just seen.

The bartender recovered enough to shout, "Hey! Stop that guy!" but after the demonstration they'd just had, the customers decided to forget all about civic duty and let the police handle this particular case.

Pendrake fled the bar and ran out into the wide corridor leading to the departure gate. The corridor swarmed with tourists hurrying to their proper gates. Three rockets were set to leave within minutes of each other. The place was pandemonium.

But if Pendrake thought that the crowd would work to his favor and hide him in its sheer numbers, he was wrong.

He hadn't taken more than ten steps before people started whispering and pointing to him.

He had been recognized.

It was only a matter of moments before somebody found a policeman and the dragnet tightened, trapping him.

He had another problem. Not only did his telepathic abilities diminish with age, they also diminished with stress. When he couldn't concentrate properly, he could not get in control of his powers.

He looked around.

Whispering.

Pointing.

A plump woman trundling up to a rent-a-cop and nodding in Pendrake's direction.

Pendrake did the only thing he could.

He ran.

He dropped the bags he had stolen and he ran.

That was all that was left to him now.

Brackett was just around the corner from Sector B when his communicator sounded the familiar (and plaintive) emergency tone.

The man identified himself as a rent-a-cop (his exact words being "civilian law-enforcement corporal") and then told Brackett how he'd just spotted Pendrake running his ass off down Sector B.

Brackett couldn't help but smile.

Matthew Pendrake was running right toward him.

Brackett drew his weapon.

And waited.

When Daily got the news about Pendrake, she was in Sector D, frantically searching among the people thronging Departure Gate F.

Now she ran, weapon drawn, toward Sector C.

When Obo got the news about Pendrake, he was in Sector A, where he'd been patiently checking out each person in a long, winding identi-card line. He'd been having no luck at all.

He felt deeply grateful when his communicator went off and the rent-a-cop informed Brackett that Pendrake was headed to Sector C.

Because now, that's just where Obo was headed, Sector C.

The big green guy loved action.

Matthew Pendrake looked like one of those tri-vid cartoon figures who came skidding to a stop so abrupt that his feet made the sounds of automobile brakes screeching to a halt.

Without his telepathic powers operating, all Pendrake had to rely on were his abilities to see, hear, and smell.

Well, just as he turned into Sector C, what he saw was this really hard-looking star cop lieutenant with his weapon drawn.

Obviously, the guy had been waiting for Pendrake. The crowd, terrified, had backed up against the walls, cowering, dreading what might happen next.

And then behind him Pendrake heard new sounds. Two more star cops: the pretty cop named Daily, and a big green Tau.

Both of them doing the same thing: cutting off any chance whatsoever of Pendrake's escape.

All three of the cops closed in.

The lieutenant was barking some order about putting his hands up and standing absolutely still.

But Pendrake wasn't paying attention.

His entire consciousness was given over to the elevator approximately twenty yards to his right, the elevator that would take him straight up into the hotel.

Did he really have any choice?

It was either hand himself over or take this one last shot at freedom, however slim.

He raced to the elevator.

Weapons burst into fire.

Crowd members screamed.

Pendrake felt a piece of flesh just above his elbow tear away, the resulting wound almost blindingly painful.

But this was his only chance.

He had to keep running.

More weapons fire.

More crowd screams.

And then, somehow, he was inside the tomb of the

elevator, jamming the heel of his right palm hard against the emergency nonstop button.

He shouted at the unseen robo-operator, "Top floor! Emergency!"

The robo-operator had no choice but to comply.

The elevator zoomed to the top floor of the hotel.

Chapter Twenty-five

All the star cops could do was dive into the doorway leading to the stairwell that wound up the center of the hotel. Brackett had heard Pendrake's shouted command to the robo-operator, so he knew just where the killer was headed.

Brackett led the way up the stairs.

"This is good exercise!" shouted Obo, two steps behind Daily.

Taus tended to put a positive spin on things. Run up twelve flights of lung-searing heart-stopping stairs? Hey, it's just the first phase of your all-new exercise program. Uh-huh.

The star cops continued banging their way to the top, the echoes of their boots on the stairs almost deafening in the narrow confines of the stairwell.

When he got off the elevator, Matthew Pendrake took in the long, beautifully carpeted corridors that stretched away to infinity on either side of him.

The doors to each suite would have every kind of burglar device imaginable on them.

A gorilla with a handful of fusion grenades would have a tough time getting inside.

He heard the clatter from deep inside the hotel; the stairwell.

Cops.

Coming up the stairs fast.

After him.

He looked around again. Nothing but empty corridors and what seemed to be miles of sealed-off doors.

He started running again, this time in an easterly direction.

Unfortunately, this time he had no idea where he was going.

By the time they reached the twelfth floor, Brackett and Daily were sheened with sweat and gasping almost pathetically for more oxygen.

Obo was whistling.

They found the elevator doors open, the car itself empty.

"He's on this floor somewhere," Brackett said, drawing his weapon. "Let's split up and try to find him."

The other two star cops nodded, Daily in between gasps, Obo in between that stupid damned cowboy song he couldn't get out of his head, "I'm a Fightin' Buckaroo, I Am, I Am."

They were from Vega, six wives of the same potentate gathered here to celebrate His Highness's sixtieth birthday, and they were just leaving their room when they saw the man.

"Oh," said one of the middle-aged but still quite decorous wives.

"Oh, my," said the second.

"It's him," said the third.

"The fugitive on the vid," said the fourth.

"Matthew," said the fifth.

"Pendrake," said the sixth.

And then, standing in the center of the corridor in a tight little cluster, they began to scream.

It was indeed Matthew Pendrake.

He had just come around the corner on his way to the stairwell, figuring to double back downstairs and genuinely baffle the star cops—when he ran into these six ladies.

Now he had no choice but to turn back, start running again.

Running . . .

"No sign of him on the east side of the floor," Brackett reported on his communicator five minutes later.

"Ditto the west side," Daily said.

"Just a minute," Obo said.

He had just started to speak into his communicator—just started to say ditto the south side—when he heard the ladies start screaming.

He ran around the corner and there they were, a cluster of them; harem ladies, he knew they were called, the "property" of some mad caliph or some such who'd been fortunate enough to inherit a sheikdom on some godforsaken planet.

As one, the six ladies screamed.

As one, the six ladies raised their arms.

As one, the six ladies pointed.

Obo followed their pointing fingers.

Pendrake had obviously just run around the corner.

Which is just where Obo was going when he heard the smashing glass.

"Obo! Obo! Where the hell are you?" Brackett shouted into his communicator.

But there was no response from Obo.

He'd obviously broken contact.

He'd obviously managed to find Matthew Pendrake.

Chapter Twenty-six

Obo found him, all right.

Obo came steaming around the corner and saw instantly what Pendrake had done—smashed through the hallway window and climbed out on the ledge that ran around the twelfth floor.

Obo got there in time to catch a glimpse of Pendrake's heel disappearing behind the curtain and the shattering silver daggers of broken glass.

He was afraid of heights.

Pendrake didn't remember that till he was out on the ledge, till he had flattened himself against the wall and was edging his way along the half-foot shelf that was the only thing that saved him from plunging to his death twelve floors below.

How small the people looked.

How distant the unyielding pavement appeared.

How crippled his heart felt, as if he could not pump sufficient blood to his body.

He was covered with cold, sticky sweat.

In order to keep inching his way along, he had to close his eyes.

And then, when he heard people below beginning to shout, he opened his eyes and looked to his right.

A Tau star cop was now on the same ledge.

Coming toward him.

My God.

• • •

Obo liked heights. He liked the birdlike feeling of standing on a ledge and letting the chill updraft of air make him feel as if he could dive into the invisible air currents and swim along, buoyed forever.

But there wasn't time for that kind of thing now.

He was here to apprehend a fugitive.

At the sudden noise below, Obo glanced down and saw that a crowd of hundreds had thronged the plaza below. They were pointing up at Obo and applauding him, or rather applauding the presence of a star cop.

Obo smiled and waved.

And then he started moving very quickly toward Pendrake.

He had no other options. He had to try it.

Seeing that the Tau was getting closer and closer, Pendrake decided to try and force the star cop to throw himself off the building.

Just as Pendrake had earlier forced the beautiful Shana to kill Ahmed.

He turned his eyes toward the star cop and began the process of mind control, which sometimes worked beautifully and other times worked not at all.

Brackett and Daily came around the corner, almost comically running head on into each other.

"Have you found Obo yet?"

"No," Brackett said. "Haven't you?"

They set off running, about to cover the only section of the floor they hadn't yet checked out.

Now, why would he have a thought like that? Obo wondered.

This was different from his thoughts of wanting to be a bird and enjoy himself as he rode along the air currents.

This was very different.

This was wanting to throw himself from the building.

And fall, tumbling, twelve floors to the shouting crowds and the pavement.

Now, why would he have a thought like that?

Pendrake could feel the mind control begin to take effect.

Feel the Tau's willpower begin to yield to his own.

Two minutes later, Brackett and Daily found themselves running into a group of six harem women just about to board an elevator.

"Around the corner!" they shouted as one. "The big green cop!" they sang.

Pendrake decided to give the Tau star cop a little test.

I want you to put one foot out in the air and let it dangle there, just as if you were going to step out in midair.

Now, there was another weird thought, Obo said to himself.

Why would he want to dangle one of his feet out in the air? A guy could get clumsy and lose his balance and—

But that's just what he did.

Leaned forward and stuck his foot out in the air and just dangled it there.

The crowd, obviously thinking he was putting on a little act for them, cheered.

"The window!" Brackett said.

Now I want you to put your hands together as if you're going to dive into a deep blue swimming pool. And then I want you to jump. Do you understand me?

Pendrake had never focused his powers harder than he did right now.

Jump.
That was a really weird thought.
Jump twelve floors down.
Splatter against the pavement.
All red blood and jutting white bone.
All rushing black death.
But oddly enough, the whole concept was starting to sound curiously *pleasant* to Obo.
Just sail right off the ledge and—
"God," Daily said, "Obo's going to jump!"

That's it. Just relax. Just put your hands together as if you're diving into a deep blue swimming pool on a very hot day. You can feel how good the cool water is on your skin. You can feel—

Brackett and Daily were now on the ledge themselves.

"Obo," Brackett said carefully, shouting above the chill, whistling wind. "He's got you in some kind of mind control. You need to fill your mind with something else. Do you understand me?"

If Obo did, he sure didn't let on.

He just stared straight down, his eyes glazed over, his huge body tensed for a plunge, like a skydiver about to jump from the plane.

"Obo, do you understand me?" Brackett said.

But he got the feeling that his big green friend didn't understand him at all.

It sure was cold up here.
It sure was high up here.
It sure was scary up here.
All Pendrake cared about now was taking the big green star cop with him.

No way Pendrake was going to escape now; but it would be fun to have company on the way down.

Most fugitives didn't get to take a star cop along for that final cosmic ride.

Brackett turned back to Daily, who was carefully inching her way along the ledge right behind Brackett. "You got any ideas?"

"Just one. That stupid song he sings."

"That cowboy song?"

"Right. 'I'm a Fightin' Buckaroo, I Am, I Am.' "

"What about it?"

"Start singing it."

"Huh?"

"If we can fill his mind with the song, maybe that'll break Pendrake's hold on his mind."

Brackett shook his head. It sounded like a pretty dumb idea.

But then Daily began singing the ditty and Brackett found himself joining in.

What the hell were they doing? Pendrake wondered. Singing at a time like this?

At first the song was just a faint, faint echo in Obo's head.

All he thought of was diving into a deep blue pool on a hot summer day.

The song barely registered.

Now I want you to lean forward even more, Obo. Get yourself ready for the big jump.

That a boy.

No; lean even farther forward.

There.

Now you're just about ready.

Just about ready.

That big blue pool is waiting for you, Obo.
Waiting for you.

"Louder!" Daily screamed at Brackett. "Sing louder!"

Boy, that pool was going to feel good.
Not just cool.
But cleansing, too.
Very cleansing.
And then, for the first time, Obo heard the song. Really heard it.
At first, he didn't respond to it.
He just kept listening to the nice, soft thoughts in his head.
Floating down to the pool. Feeling cool and clean and peaceful.
But then he couldn't help himself.
Much as he wanted to keep his mind totally fixed on the concept of the nice blue swimming pool, he started muttering along with the song.
"I'm a fightin' buckaroo, I am, I am."

"He's singing!" Daily shouted. "Listen!"

What the hell was this "I'm a fightin' buckaroo, I am, I am" stuff anyway, Pendrake wondered.
He was losing control.
Not all at once.
But gradually.
The big green cop was singing along and—
Pendrake decided to give it one more try.
He closed his eyes and focused all his power on Obo.
It's time now, Obo. Time to dive into that deep blue pool.
Now, Obo.
Now.

• • •

Brackett jerked as he saw Obo start to lean forward on the very tip of the edge.

Obviously, despite their singing, Pendrake was still in control of Obo's mind.

If Brackett fired and killed Pendrake, Obo would pitch right down twelve floors with him.

All Brackett could do was wait his chance.

And keep singing.

He bellowed, "I'm a fightin' buckaroo, I am, I am."

Now, Obo.
Jump now.

But then in a gush, a geyser, the song came up in Obo, and he began singing with almost operatic glee, "I'm a fightin' buckaroo, I am, I am."

And then he looked down and saw how close he was to pitching over the side.

And then he glanced over at Pendrake and realized that he'd been under the man's sway somehow.

And then Brackett said, "Now!"

And both Brackett and Daily opened up, firing not at Pendrake but around him, beams of searing blue light meant to imprison him on the very edge of the ledge.

But Pendrake obviously had other ideas.

He flung his arms wide and screamed and then did just what he'd wanted Obo to do.

He hurled himself off the ledge.

The crowd scattered, giving him plenty of room to splatter.

Chapter Twenty-seven

Brackett had never administered the Steelman Probe before to anybody who was essentially just a puddle of blood, smashed bones, and loose organs.

But at least the meds got Pendrake covered up enough so that finally all Brackett had to look at was Pendrake's forehead.

Too bad they couldn't do anything about the smell.

Brackett got to work.

Captain Carnes had arrived on the scene just as Pendrake was tumbling downward from the twelfth floor. In all, it was a pretty spectacular display. Carnes was just happy that it was not one of his cops who'd been tumbling from the ledge up there.

Now, Carnes stood twenty feet away from where Brackett was applying the Steelman on the corpse. The crowd had been halved. After all, the most compelling part of the show, seeing the man actually fall and splatter, was over. Now there were other kicks to seek out.

Next to Carnes stood Daily and Obo.

Carnes said, nodding in the direction of Brackett, "He won't get anything."

"No?" Daily said.

Carnes shook his head. "Not when a man's been traumatized that much at death."

Obo said, "Look."

"I'll be damned," Carnes said.

The way Brackett had suddenly leaned over, you could tell he was getting something.

In all, Brackett spent thiry-two minutes kneeling next to Pendrake, the styluslike tool held firmly to the dead man's forehead.

When he was done, Brackett replaced the tool in the small leather bag where it belonged.

For some reason, Brackett did not look at all happy.

He walked over to Captain Carnes and the other two and said, "Well, I found out one thing, anyway."

"What's that?" Carnes said.

"Ahmed had actually developed himself into a low-grade telepath, enough so that he realized who and what Pendrake really was, which scared Pendrake quite a lot. And that's why Pendrake coerced Shana into killing Ahmed."

"So that's why," Daily said.

"Anything else?" Carnes said.

And here, Brackett looked very strange, almost sad. "Yes, one other thing. But I'll tell you about that a little later."

And with that, with no nod of head, with no good-bye of any kind, he left the plaza with its vulture-like gawkers and shattered corpse and three very curious star cops.

Brackett had one more appointment to keep before this case was finally closed.

Chapter Twenty-eight

"A lot of excitement this morning," Marcia Tenhold said.

She looked young and quietly seductive in a red-and-white checkered cowgirl shirt and some nice-fitting cowgirl jeans.

She was in the bedroom, packing her bags.

He leaned against the doorframe, managing to look both angry and sad.

Sensing something wrong, she looked up. "Are you all right, Brackett?"

Why wouldn't I be all right?"

"You're just so . . . quiet."

"Maybe it's because I think I should arrest you."

Her head snapped up from the bag she'd been plumping down. "Arrest me? Are you joking, Brackett?"

"You know what a Steelman Probe is?"

"Of course."

"Well, I just performed one on our mutual friend Pendrake. And guess what?"

"I'm sure you're going to tell me."

"Before he worked for Dirk St. Romaine, he bummed around the beaches of Trallagar. Some very trendy people there."

"I wouldn't know."

"Oh, sure you would, Marcia. As the daughter of a rich man, Trallagar was almost your inherited right. And you spent a lot of time there with our friend Pendrake. And that's where you came up with the idea to have him read your father's mind and find some scandal you could use against the old man so you could destroy him—and come into a nice fat inheritance all for yourself."

For a time she said nothing . . . then her dark eyes grew even darker with tears. "You don't know what life with him was like, Brackett. When I was nine years old, he came into my room one night and he—"

"I'm sorry," Brackett said. "Maybe you had a good reason to do what you did."

"He killed himself. I didn't kill him. He was afraid of the scandal. There's nothing you can hold me for."

"I know there's not. But I just wanted to let you know that I knew how it was your father came to kill himself."

"Don't judge me, Brackett. You don't know me well enough to judge me."

Brackett sighed. "You're probably right, Marcia. I probably don't know you well enough."

He turned to leave.

"I really did want to sleep with you last night, Brackett. I like you. I really do."

He wanted to say the same, that he liked her despite what she'd done, but somehow he couldn't form the proper words.

He looked at her a last time and said, "So long, Marcia."

And then he was gone.

All the way down in the elevator, he kept thinking of what she'd felt like in his arms last night. It had been a long time since he'd felt that kind of tenderness.

Suddenly, he wanted to be back on the precinct ship, headed out to a different sector.

He wished people were honest. But then, he wished a lot of things.

When he reached the ground floor, he hurried to catch up with the other star cops.

Chapter Twenty-nine

They were in the lounge, Daily explaining to Obo how clever Pendrake had been in disguising himself as the small man in the black suit that the eyewitness had seen leaving St. Romaine's cabin, when Brackett came in and sat down with them.

"You look tired," Daily said.

"I guess I probably am," Brackett said.

"It's nice to be back on the 107th," Daily said. "Sometimes I worry that eventually I'll prefer life aboard ship to real life planetside. You know, the way Carnes is."

Brackett smiled. "That's one thing you'll never have to worry about."

"Huh?"

"Being like Carnes. Right, Obo?"

Now it was Obo's turn to smile. "Thank God, there's only one egg-suckin' guy like him in the whole Federation."

"I forgot," Brackett said, "Obo learned a new word while we were planetside."

"Egg-suckin'." Daily laughed. "And it's such a nice word, too." Then she frowned. "Carnes said you've answered all the questions in your report."

"I tried," Brackett said. Then he thought about Marcia Tenhold, how it had felt to dance with her, to hold her. He may have answered all the other questions but he hadn't answered the basic one: why so many human beings lied to themselves and each other.

Brackett spent the next few minutes summarizing the case.

All the while Brackett talked, Obo hummed under his breath, "I'm a Fightin' Buckaroo, I am, I am."

About the time Brackett was finishing up, Dreesen appeared in the archway. He looked reluctant to approach Daily. He'd never looked sadder.

She decided to make things easy for him. She excused herself and went over to Dreesen.

Up close, he looked even sadder.

"Would you walk with me?" he said.

"Sure."

They ambled down the corridor, nodding to people who passed by.

"I'm leaving tomorrow," he said.

"Leaving?"

"I just talked to Carnes. I didn't tell him why but I told him that for personal reasons, I wanted a transfer. There's an opening on the 106th that I qualify for. So I took it."

She should feel happy, or at least relieved, Daily reasoned, but somehow she felt neither.

"You're a very nice man, Dreesen."

"I really do love you, Daily."

"I know. And I'm flattered. I really am. It's just—"

"It's just that you want a career, and I want three point two kids." He smiled sadly.

"I never have figured out how that works," Daily said. "That three-point-two business, I mean."

And then they stopped right in the middle of the corridor, people flowing around them, and he kissed her. It was so sweet and so tender that she started crying herself, and she didn't care who saw her crying or what they thought about it.

"I'm going to miss you Dreesen," she said.

• • •

Five minutes later, when Daily returned to the table with Brackett and Obo, the two star cops were watching the vid.

There was Wade Foster, cowboy getup and all, talking to kids everywhere.

"It's good to see him back in the saddle again," Obo said. "I missed him." He sounded like a very enthusiastic six-year-old.

Brackett looked over at Daily and smiled.

The human mind would never be able to grasp the Tau mind.

Never.

DAVID DRAKE

__NORTHWORLD 0-441-84830-3/$4.99
The consensus ruled twelve hundred worlds—but not Northworld. Three fleets had been dispatched to probe the enigma of Northworld. None returned. Now, Commissioner Nils Hansen must face the challenge of the distant planet. There he will confront a world at war, a world of androids...all unique, all lethal.

__NORTHWORLD 2: VENGEANCE 0-441-58615-5/$4.95
__NORTHWORD 3: JUSTICE 0-441-58616-3/$4.99

__SURFACE ACTION 0-441-36375-X/$4.50
Venus has been transformed into a world of underwater habitats for Earth's survivors. Battles on Venus must be fought on the ocean's exotic surface. Johnnie Gordon trained his entire life for battle, and now his time has come to live a warrior's life on the high seas.

THE FLEET Edited by David Drake and Bill Fawcett
The soldiers of the Human/Alien Alliance come from different worlds and different cultures. But they share a common mission: to reclaim occupied space from the savage Khalian invaders.

    __BREAKTHROUGH 0-441-24105-0/$3.95
    __COUNTERATTACK 0-441-24104-2/$3.95
    __SWORN ALLIES 0-441-24090-9/$3.95
    __TOTAL WAR 0-441-24093-3/$3.95
    __CRISIS 0-441-24106-9/$4.50